S0-BSE-600

THE MISSING
MOVIE CREATURE

OTHER YEARLING BOOKS YOU WILL ENJOY:

THE HAIRY BEAST IN THE WOODS, Mary Anderson
THE TERRIBLE THING IN THE BOTTLE,
Mary Anderson
THE CURSE OF THE DEMON, Mary Anderson
THE HAUNTING OF HILLCREST, Mary Anderson
THE LEIPZIG VAMPIRE, Mary Anderson
TERROR UNDER THE TENT, Mary Anderson
THE THREE SPIRITS OF VANDERMEER MANOR,
Mary Anderson
PRISONER OF VAMPIRES, Nancy Garden
THE HEADLESS CUPID, Zilpha Keatley Snyder
THE WITCHES OF WORM, Zilpha Keatley Snyder

YEARLING BOOKS/YOUNG YEARLINGS/YEARLING CLASSICS
are designed especially to entertain and enlighten
young people. Patricia Reilly Giff, consultant to
this series, received the bachelor's degree from
Marymount College. She holds the master's degree
in history from St. John's University, and a Profes-
sional Diploma in Reading from Hofstra University.
She was a teacher and reading consultant for many
years, and is the author of numerous books for
young readers.

For a complete listing of all Yearling titles, write to
Dell Readers Service, P.O. Box 1045,
South Holland, IL 60473.

MOSTLY MONSTERS

THE MISSING MOVIE CREATURE

Mary Anderson

A YEARLING BOOK

Published by
Dell Publishing
a division of
Bantam Doubleday Dell Publishing Group, Inc.
666 Fifth Avenue
New York, New York 10103

Copyright © 1989 by Mary Anderson

All rights reserved. No part of this book may be reproduced or transmitted in any form or by any means, electronic or mechanical, including photocopying, recording, or by any information storage and retrieval system, without the written permission of the Publisher, except where permitted by law.

The trademark Yearling® is registered in the U.S. Patent and Trademark Office.

ISBN: 0-440-40181-X

Printed in the United States of America

June 1989

10 9 8 7 6 5 4 3 2

CWO

Chapter One

CASSIE HASTINGS WAS STARVING. SHE RAN DOWN THE stairs of Ludlington Manor and hurried into the dining room for breakfast. But when she saw the first course, she frowned. "Not grapefruit!" Cassie knew that grapefruit for breakfast meant Oliver Crenshaw was coming. "Crenshaw is the only person in the world who likes grapefruit."

Cassie's cousin, Barney Prescott, was already seated at the table, plucking the cherry from his portion. "I can't stand this stuff either." He puckered his lips then swallowed a bite. "If scientists can do so much, why can't they make grapefruit taste good?"

Aunt Alex took her seat at the head of the table. "Good boy, Barney; you should get accustomed to many different tastes in life. But you should also wait until guests have arrived before eating."

Cassie pushed her plate aside. "I'll never get accustomed to grapefruit—or to Crenshaw. Neither one is to my taste."

"Do we have to wait?" asked Barney. "After all, Crenshaw is our tutor, so he's not really a guest."

Aunt Alex unfolded her linen napkin. "True, but Ollie is also my business manager and my very dear friend so it's only polite we wait until he arrives."

During the short time Cassie and Barney had been living with their great-aunt, they'd learned she was a caring, generous woman. Alexandra Ludlington was also one of the richest women in the country. In addition, Barney thought she was one of the nicest. Cassie liked Aunt Alex, too, but she couldn't warm up to Crenshaw and didn't want to try.

Cassie glanced longingly at the silver platter overflowing with blueberry pancakes. "They'll get cold," she complained. "Why is Crenshaw coming so early today? Our lessons don't begin until ten o'clock."

"This is a *business* breakfast," said Aunt Alex brightly. "All the financial bigwigs have them. Since you'll both be living with me all year you should learn about business matters."

2

"And *money*," added Oliver Crenshaw, rushing into the room out of breath. He handed his overcoat to Nora, the housekeeper, then hurried toward the breakfast table. "Teach those children all about money, Alex. They've got to learn squandering a penny is a sin they'll regret the rest of their lives."

Barney scooped up some pancakes. "Aunt Alex says she has more money than there are fishes in the sea."

Crenshaw adjusted his shirt cuffs, buffed his gold pocket watch, straightened his silk tie, then sat down. "Perhaps that won't be true forever," he said ominously. "There are certain people out in California who seem determined to turn your great-aunt into a *pauper*."

Cassie's appetite suddenly vanished. "You haven't lost all your money, have you, Aunt Alex?" she asked with concern. That might mean Cassie would have to return to boarding school immediately and Cassie *hated* boarding school.

Aunt Alex chuckled. "Of course I haven't, silly. I can't possibly lose all my money because I'm *diversified*. My money is in oil wells, baby powder, computers, who knows what else. Ollie makes sure the Ludlington wealth is spread over various investments."

"My dad says it's not polite to talk about money at the table," Barney observed.

"That depends on the amount of money, young man," Crenshaw replied. "When it's in the millions it can be discussed *anywhere*. Millions always supersede etiquette, remember that."

"Nonsense, Ollie," Aunt Alex scolded. "Tell Barney you were only joking."

"I'm in no mood for jokes, Alex," said Crenshaw gruffly. "As your business manager, it's my job to take money matters *seriously*. By my calculations, you're losing exactly thirty-seven thousand dollars per day and that's no joking matter!"

"That's impossible," said Barney. "No one can lose that much money."

"What's happening to it?" asked Cassie. "Where's it going?"

"Who knows!" Crenshaw shouted. "Maybe it's going up in smoke or getting thrown down a rat hole!" He placed his briefcase on the table and removed several documents. "These are the monthly production costs from Clarion Pictures. They're spending money as if it's going out of style. *Your* money, Alex."

"*Mine?*"

"Yes, you're a major stockholder in Clarion Pictures. Their latest film is already a million over budget. I've spoken with David Douglas, the head of the studio, I've called accounting, but I can't

4

get a straight answer. It's all very mysterious. There's a *conspiracy* going on out there!"

Cassie reached for some pancakes. "They're cold. I'll ask Nora to make fresh ones."

"Don't you dare," Crenshaw insisted. "There's too much waste in the world already. Didn't your parents ever teach you *thriftiness*?"

Cassie gave Crenshaw a filthy look. What a rotten stupid question! He knew perfectly well she'd been ignored by her parents—shipped off to fancy French boarding schools since the age of six. "No, they didn't teach me anything!"

"My mom taught *me* to be thrifty," said Barney, never missing a chance to show up Cassie. "I eat everything on my plate."

"Did she also teach you to be obnoxious?" Cassie asked. "This entire subject makes me *très ennuyée*–which means *bored*, for your information."

Aunt Alex peered over her eyeglasses, then tapped the table with her spoon. "Children, behave yourselves. It's foolish to argue about *pancakes*." She handed the tray to her housekeeper. "Nora, please warm these up." Then she poured Crenshaw some coffee. "Your figures must be wrong, Ollie. I *can't* be losing that much money."

Crenshaw looked offended. "My figures are *never* wrong. I've taken care of the Ludlington fortune for years, but if you don't trust my judgment . . ."

5

"Calm down," soothed Aunt Alex. "Your judgment is impeccable, Ollie, and we'd be lost without you. We count on you for *everything*, isn't that right, children?"

Cassie gritted her teeth in silence.

Barney nodded.

Crenshaw nervously sipped his coffee. "I hate not knowing where your money is going, Alex, but I'll get to the bottom of this. I'm personally flying out to California tomorrow. After a few days in Hollywood I'll have everything straightened out, don't worry."

"Why should I worry?" said Aunt Alex. "In fact, I think I'll come along. It's time I took a more active interest in business."

"What about us?" asked Barney. "I'd love to see Hollywood. Can we come along, too?"

"Naturally," said Aunt Alex. "Remember our agreement? The four of us will spend the entire year together, going wherever the winds take us. Right now, the winds are taking us to Hollywood!"

Chapter Two

BARNEY EAGERLY STARED OUT THE WINDOW OF THE airplane. "When we get to Hollywood, let's go on all the tours, see all the TV studios, eat in fancy restaurants, and get invited to celebrity parties, okay?"

Traveling was no novelty for Cassie, but meeting movie stars would be a new event. "I wouldn't mind bumping into a few celebrities," she admitted.

"We won't have time for that," warned Crenshaw. "Remember, this is a *business* trip."

"Nonsense, the children will have lots of time for fun." Aunt Alex added, "There's *always* time for fun, Ollie."

"No, there isn't," he stated. "Watch out, Alex, don't let the children get caught up in the glamor

7

of Hollywood. Make them realize movie-making is a business that requires hard work, long hours, and discipline."

"That's silly," said Cassie. "Movies are made by celebrities who don't wake up until noon."

"How much longer before we arrive?" asked Barney. "I can hardly wait. How about you, Cassie?"

Cassie shrugged. "Don't behave like a common *tourist*, Prescott. Remember, gawking at stars is *très bourgeois*."

Barney ignored her. "Where will we stay? Lots of big stars have beach houses in Malibu. Maybe we could stay out there and go belly-surfing with them!"

Cassie groaned. "Aunt Alex, tell Barney to behave. Can't you make him learn finesse or teach him style? What if he makes a major faux pas? I'll die of embarrassment!"

Aunt Alex smiled sympathetically. "I'll keep an eye on him, dear."

"Don't bother," Barney snapped. "I know about style. That's what movie stars have—the ones in the big mansions in Beverly Hills and Bel Air. I learned about it on that TV show *The Rich and Their Riches*. Hey, will *we* stay in a mansion, too?"

"No," said Crenshaw, "we'll stay in a hotel close to the movie studio."

"With twenty-four-hour room service?" he asked hopefully.

"Careful," Crenshaw warned, "don't become a hedonist."

"What's that?" asked Barney.

"Someone who lives totally for pleasure."

"Hey, that's for me. Aunt Al promised this would be my year of fun and adventure."

Aunt Alex laughed. "And I always keep my promises, so it's a deal. Let's do all the things tourists do, okay, Barney? We'll visit Knott's Berry Farm, take bus tours to the movie stars' homes. Oh, I wonder if the Brown Derby is still open, what a fun place to lunch." She glanced out the window dreamily. "I wonder if Hollywood is as wonderfully romantic as ever."

"Have you been there before?" asked Cassie.

"Yes, dear," she said, "but it was long, long ago."

"I'll bet you were there with Hugo, right?" asked Barney. He loved hearing stories of all the places Aunt Alex and her late husband, Hugo, had been.

"No, not with Hugo," Aunt Alex replied vaguely.

"But we'll do *everything*, right?" asked Barney.

"I promised, didn't I?" said Aunt Alex. "We'll have ourselves a splendid time. We'll paint the town! It'll be a fantastic pleasure trip."

"It's a *business* trip," Crenshaw argued. He

glanced out the window as the Los Angeles skyline came into view. "The people at Clarion Pictures will soon learn that money doesn't grow on palm trees!"

At the airport Barney glanced around, hoping to spy celebrities on their way somewhere but he didn't. Cassie put on her sunglasses, hoping she'd be mistaken for a movie star but she wasn't.

After Crenshaw had claimed their luggage, a nervous young man approached them. His left eye twitched uncontrollably and his hands shook. "Are you Oliver Crenshaw? I have a limousine waiting outside for you and Mrs. Ludlington. Welcome to Hollywood. My name is Albert Orwell, I'm Mr. Douglas's assistant."

Crenshaw looked displeased. "Where's David Douglas? He promised to meet us in person. Mrs. Ludlington is a major stockholder and deserves personal attention."

Albert Orwell cringed. "I know," he said meekly. "Mr. Douglas planned to come himself but there've been problems at the studio."

"What kinds of problems?" asked Aunt Alex.

Albert sighed. "*All* kinds. Something awful happens every day. Lately, employees are afraid to show up for work. I think they're convinced the place is *jinxed*." Albert's eye twitched frantically.

"The troubles began when we started making that horror movie. Things ran smoothly at Clarion Pictures until we began shooting *The Monster Master*."

Aunt Alex grew upset. "A *horror* movie? Ollie, you never told me Clarion Pictures makes horror movies. I never would've invested my money if I'd known that. I *hate* horror movies; they poison people's minds."

Cassie *loved* gory movies. At boarding school she'd often sneak from class and take a taxi into town to see one. Later, she'd scare everyone in her dorm with vivid descriptions of the most disgusting scenes. "Horror movies are great, Aunt Alex, and they make lots of money."

"So what?" she replied. "Just because people love to be scared, *I* don't want to scare them. Ollie, why did you invest my money in Clarion Pictures when you know how I feel about those movies?"

"I was told Clarion PIctures *didn't* make horror movies," Crenshaw protested. "There must be some mistake."

Albert shrugged. "There's no mistake, sir. *The Monster Master* is a multimillion-dollar horror movie. Maybe I shouldn't say this, but—well—there's something eerie about the whole project. Normally, I'm not a superstitious person but I'm beginning to believe the rumors. Maybe there's a jinx on this project. Do you believe in such things, Mrs. Ludlington?"

"Of course not, I believe in common sense."

"So do I," Albert agreed, "and common sense tells me there's some awful mystery at Clarion Pictures."

"Then let's get out there and *solve* it," said Crenshaw.

"Yes, come along," Aunt Alex agreed. "Let's not keep Hollywood waiting."

Chapter Three

WHEN BARNEY TOOK A LOOK AT THE STRETCH LIMO waiting for them, his eyes nearly popped. "Look, the seats are covered in snakeskin and there's a TV and a bar in back. Isn't that fantastic?"

"Fantastically *wasteful*," said Crenshaw. "Such luxuries subtract from company profits."

Barney didn't care. He leaned back to enjoy the VIP treatment. As the chauffeur drove through the city, Barney checked the well-stocked bar and poured himself some ginger ale. "Look, there's crushed ice back here, too. I'm going to *love* Hollywood."

Albert sat silently twitching. Cassie had never seen anyone so nervous. He looked frightened, too. Of what? she wondered. Could Clarion Pictures really be *jinxed*?

Aunt Alex pointed toward the entrance of the movie studio. "Look, children, we've arrived."

As the limousine approached the gateway of Clarion Pictures, two huge gilded griffins above the iron doors came into view. The gates parted and three uniformed guards ushered the car through the barricaded driveway. As the gates slammed shut behind them, a remote-control alarm announced their car was approaching the main building.

"The only thing missing is a *moat*," said Crenshaw. "Why is there such heavy security around here?"

"Orders from Mr. Douglas," Albert explained. "Ever since the troubles began, we've been extra cautious."

"Why? What's been happening here?" asked Aunt Alex. "Give us *details*."

Albert was evasive. "You'll have to discuss that with David Douglas; I'm only an assistant."

Cassie had a feeling Albert was *afraid* to reveal the details.

Barney was so busy enjoying himself, he didn't notice anything. He poured another soda and switched on the TV.

"Stop fiddling with everything," Cassie complained. "This isn't an amusement park ride."

"It's *better*," said Barney. "Movie moguls know how to live!" He picked up the cellular phone. "Can I call my mom on this thing?"

"You can call her this evening from the hotel," said Aunt Alex, taking the phone away.

"Act your age," Cassie pleaded.

"I will if you will," said Barney. "You're only two years older, not twenty."

"But you're being so *childish*," she argued. As the limousine drove past the soundstages and back lots, Cassie leaned out the window. "It looks deserted. Where is everyone?"

"We had to shut down a few productions because of financial problems," Albert explained. "Right now, *The Monster Master* is a our biggest project, so the studio is banking on it."

"Hey, how come there are no actors in cowboy hats, togas, tights, and tutus?" asked Barney. "I thought we'd see tons of movie stars falling over each other."

"Calm down," said Cassie, poking him. "Have some sophistication. Remember, gawking at movie stars on back lots is *très passé*."

"The actors are inside on the sets right now," said Albert, "but don't worry, you'll see lots of movie stars."

15

"Big stars?" asked Barney.

"Superstars?" asked Cassie.

"Well, things are lots different than they were back in the glory days of Hollywood," Albert admitted. "Years ago, Clarion Pictures' motto was 'We have more stars than the sky.' Those were the great old days when Gordon Douglas was head of the studio. G.D. was known as the Terror of Tinseltown. Every actor in Hollywood feared him but every actor wanted to work for him. His son, David, has tried hard to carry on that tradition."

"Everyone fears him too?" asked Barney.

Albert twitched. "No, only me," he admitted.

As the limousine stopped outside the executive offices of Clarion Pictures, the alarm rang to announce their arrival. When they walked into the building, a guard carefully checked Albert's ID badge before allowing them into the elevator.

"I'll bet the CIA has less security," said Crenshaw. "I don't understand this."

"Perhaps Mr. Douglas is a nervous man," Aunt Alex suggested.

The elevator doors opened and a very nervous receptionist greeted them. Then a very nervous secretary ushered them toward David Douglas's private office.

"Everyone looks ready for a breakdown," Crenshaw observed.

David Douglas hurried from his office to greet them. He was a short, pudgy man with a small bald spot and a giant cigar. "Dear lady, dear lady, dear lady," he said, grabbing Aunt Alex by the hand, "it's an honor to meet you. Come into my office." He guided them past the plush red carpeting into his huge executive suite.

Barney had never seen a desk so big. As he sank into an easy chair, he nearly disappeared inside the cushions.

Cassie glanced at the life-size photos of famous movie stars on the walls. "I finally feel I'm in Hollywood," she said, sighing.

David Douglas nodded. "Yes, the greatest stars of the silver screen are up there. The biggest, the best, the legendary: They all worked for Dad. He was famous in this town. Everyone loved him."

"That's not what *we* heard," said Barney with his usual candor. "We heard he was called the Terror of Tinseltown."

David Douglas scowled. "Who told you that?" he asked, glancing at Albert, who sat twitching in the corner. "Well, that was a term of endearment. Everyone *loved* Dad. Dad built this studio from rock heaps and clay pits and made it great. Over the years, his movies collected eighty-three Academy Awards! And Clarion Pictures can do it again,

17

I promise you. You have your money well invested, Mrs. Ludlington, never fear."

"I'm not so sure," said Aunt Alex.

"Why are you overbudget?" asked Crenshaw.

David Douglas chewed nervously on the end of his cigar. "We've had a few accidents lately. Actually, we've had *lots* of accidents. But that can happen to anyone."

"What kinds of accidents?" asked Aunt Alex.

David Douglas grew evasive. "Dear lady, why bother yourself with such details?"

"What kinds of accidents?" Crenshaw persisted.

"All kinds," he admitted. "Big ones, small ones, you name it, it's happened. If I were a superstitious person, I'd think we were—"

"Jinxed?" asked Cassie.

"But I'm not a superstitious person," he continued. "Things will work out. Sometimes, production problems occur quite unexpectedly. I'm getting things under control, I assure you. Return home and relax, Mrs. Ludlington."

"Don't pull wool over these old eyes, Mr. Douglas," replied Aunt Alex. "What are you trying to hide?"

"Yes, what's the trouble here?" asked Crenshaw. "We've been told your problems began with that horror movie."

David Douglas began pulling at his skimpy hair.

"Yes, that's when things started going wrong. That movie has turned into a nightmare! I've tried to hush things up so people wouldn't panic, but it's been one disaster after another."

"Why don't you close down production?" asked Crenshaw.

"I *can't*, that movie is our only potential blockbuster. If we close down *The Monster Master*, we'll lose millions!"

"Does that mean Aunt A. will lose more money, too?" asked Barney.

"Exactly," said David Douglas helplessly. "All our investors would lose a fortune. I'm between a rock and a hard place, so somehow we'll have to continue until the movie is completed."

"But it's a *horror* movie," Aunt Alex argued. "I don't want my money invested in slime creatures!"

David Douglas took some bicarbonate from his desk, mixed it into ice water, then drank it. He belched discreetly. "*The Monster Master* didn't start out as a horror movie," he explained. "When we bought Professor Ratoff's book, it was called *The Monster Syndrome*. Real egghead stuff, you know? Let's face it, that isn't commercial, so we had to make some changes."

"Victor Ratoff is a serious scientist," said Crenshaw. "How does he feel about your changes?"

David Douglas belched again. "He hates them,

but who cares? I've put Ratoff on salary as a screenwriter and given him his own office. Besides, he has *screen credit*. Most people would *kill* for screen credit!"

"No, I don't like it," Aunt Alex repeated. "I don't want my money financing one of those—*smasher* movies."

"They're called *slasher* movies," Cassie corrected.

"Or *splatter* movies," Barney added.

"That's even worse!" said Aunt Alex.

"But this movie is *classy* horror," David Douglas assured her. "All the blood and gore is very tasteful, believe me."

"The mere idea of it makes me feel all crawly," said Aunt Alex. "I pity the poor young actors who have to work in such swill. I'm sure they'd be happier sweeping streets!"

"No, we have a real classy *old* star," David Douglas explained. "Basil Trelawny has come out of retirement to play the scientist who brings the monster to life."

Suddenly, Aunt Alex got a peculiar expression on her face. Her eyes had a strange faraway look and her mouth began to tremble. "Did you say *Basil Trelawny*?" she asked faintly.

"That's right," said David Douglas. "Basil Trelawny was quite a superstar years ago—a real heartthrob in his day."

Aunt Alex grew dizzy. "I know," she said, gasping for breath.

Crenshaw grabbed her arm. "Is something wrong, Alex? You look so pale."

"I'm all right," she insisted, "but I never thought I'd hear that name again."

"You mean Basil Trelawny?" asked Barney.

"Do you know him?" asked Crenshaw.

Aunt Alex didn't answer. She took a hankie from her purse and patted her forehead. "I think we should leave now," she said faintly.

"No, we can't go yet," said Crenshaw. "We need to have a conference and meet with the company's executives."

"I'm leaving," Aunt Alex insisted, and got up.

"Alex, you may be facing financial ruin!"

"I don't care, Ollie. Some things in this world are more important than money and this is one of them."

"*What* is?"

"Never mind," she snapped. "It's not your business!"

Barney had never seen Aunt Alex behave so strangely. And he'd never heard her be *rude* to Crenshaw!

Crenshaw looked surprised and offended. "I don't understand."

"Come along, children," Aunt Alex insisted.

"Let's check into our hotel." She shook hands with David Douglas, then quickly brushed past Crenshaw on her way toward the door.

"What's wrong with Aunt Alex?" Barney whispered.

Cassie shrugged. "I can't figure it out," she answered.

Chapter Four

BARNEY STARED OUT THE HOTEL ROOM WINDOW TOWARD the pool below. "Do you think there are any movie stars down there?"

"Don't be idiotic," said Cassie. "Celebrities have their own pools. Only tourists hang out at poolside."

Barney sat on the bed and sipped his strawberry ice-cream soda with butter brickle–chip ice cream.

"Where'd you get that?" asked Cassie.

"From room service, it's my second." He slurped up the last strawful. "How will we meet movie stars?"

"Don't worry, I have it figured out. We'll get a special pass for the soundstage. That way, we'll get personal introductions and VIP treatment.

23

Maybe the stars will invite us into their trailers for lunch. After all, a person should do things in grand luxe style."

"Can Aunt Alex arrange that?"

"Why not? She's a major stockholder and money talks."

"Maybe so," said Barney, "but Aunt Alex won't talk. She hasn't said a word since we checked in."

"It has something to do with that actor Basil Trelawny," said Cassie. "Aunt Alex acted peculiar when she heard his name. Isn't that mysterious?"

Barney agreed. "That's not the only mystery. People at Clarion Pictures acted weird, too.

There was a knock on the door. "How are your rooms?" asked Crenshaw, coming in.

"Mine is great," said Barney. "I've got a terrific view of the swimming pool."

"And how is your Aunt Alex feeling?" he asked.

"She's acting weird," said Barney. "Know what she's doing right now? Resting."

"Resting?" asked Crenshaw with concern. "No, Alex never rests during the day. She can outrun anyone half her age. I hope she hasn't caught a virus. I *told* her to get a flu shot last month but she paid no attention. A person her age should *always* get a flu shot!"

"Hey, you don't think she's really *sick*, do you?" asked Barney.

Without knocking, Aunt Alex entered the room. "Who are you talking about?" she asked. "Who's sick?"

"*You* are," said Barney. "Crenshaw said so. He said a person your age should always have shots."

Aunt Alex glared at Crenshaw. "Do you think I'm so *old*? I'm scarcely six months older than you, Oliver Crenshaw!"

"No, that's not what I said," he protested. "I mean, it's not what I meant."

"I never trust a man who doesn't mean what he says," she replied, "or say what he means."

"You mean you're all right?" asked Cassie.

"I'm perfectly fine, thank you. I just came in to see if you children had unpacked yet."

"I unpacked everything," said Barney proudly.

"That's too bad," she replied, "because you'll have to pack it all up again. I've decided we're going back home."

"But why?" asked Cassie.

"I don't think we should stay here in Hollywood. This place is a bad influence."

"But we have *business* here," Crenshaw protested.

"You can attend to the business," she told him. "I'm taking the children back home immediately."

"You can't do that," Barney argued. "You said we'd take a bus tour, go to a berry farm, and eat lunch in a hat. You *promised*."

"Did I say *all that*?" asked Aunt Alex.

"Yes, you did," said Cassie, "on the airplane."

Aunt Alex sighed. "I'm afraid I don't remember. Maybe I *am* getting old." She began pacing the room. "Now isn't this a pretty pickle? I can't break a promise."

"Then *stay*," said Crenshaw.

"No, I can't stay," she protested, "not if . . ." Her voice trailed off to a whisper as she paced back and forth. "Oh, all right," she finally said, "a promise is a promise, so we'll stay. But don't blame me if this entire trip turns out to be a disappointment, Ollie." She hurried toward the door. "A terrible, heartbreaking, bitter disappointment!" she added, then slammed the door behind her.

"No, wait," Crenshaw pleaded, quickly hurrying after her.

"What was all *that* about?" asked Barney, scratching his head.

The next morning as Aunt Alex, Crenshaw, and the children walked down the ninth-floor corridor of Clarion Pictures, people peeked out of the offices then quickly slammed their doors.

"Why is everyone so frightened?" asked Cassie.

"Word must be out," said Crenshaw. "They know a major stockholder is snooping around.

Maybe everyone is afraid of losing their job. And maybe they should be. Maybe this studio should close down production of *The Monster Master*. Maybe I'll speak to David Douglas about it."

Aunt Alex grabbed Crenshaw's arm. "No, Ollie, don't do that. You can't put people out of work, especially not—"

"Not who?" asked Crenshaw.

"Never mind, I just can't be present for such a meeting. In fact," she added, "I won't be."

"What's that mean?"

"It means I have another appointment," she replied.

"No, you haven't," Crenshaw argued.

"Yes, I have," Aunt Alex insisted, hurrying back toward the elevator. "Don't worry, I'll meet you all in the commissary for lunch at one o'clock. See you then, bye."

"Wait, Alex, don't go," Crenshaw pleaded.

Ignoring his objections, Aunt Alex disappeared into the elevator and was gone.

"What's wrong with Aunt A. lately?" asked Barney.

"I can't figure it," Cassie admitted, "but I know what's wrong with Crenshaw. I figured that out last night. I'm certain that Crenshaw is secretly—"

"Enough talk," Crenshaw interrupted, grabbing each child by the arm. "You two wait here in the

27

lounge during my meeting—and don't get underfoot."

"We're not waiting *here*," Cassie argued. "We
want VIP passes. We want to tour the soundstages."

"I brought my autograph book," said Barney.

"Absolutely not," said Crenshaw firmly. "You
can't hold up movie production to get autographs.
Does money grow on trees? No! We're enough
overbudget already, so just sit here and wait until
I return."

"What made him so *angry*?" Barney wondered.
As Crenshaw left, he watched the executives gather
in the outer lobby. When they had all assembled,
Crenshaw led them into David Douglas's office.
Barney slumped into the lounge sofa. "If we'd
stayed at the hotel, at least we could've taken a
swim. It's no fun coming here if we can't see
movie stars."

"We'll see stars," said Cassie.

"How? Crenshaw won't authorize a pass."

"He will," said Cassie with sly determination,
"just wait."

Barney knew Cassie's reputation for doing
sneaky, foul, rotten things. "Can you make Crenshaw change his mind? How?"

"I'll think of something," she said, "just wait."

As Barney watched Cassie, he pictured the

wheels turning in her mind. If anyone could trick Crenshaw, it was Cassie!

After a while, an old man wearing thick bifocals came hurrying into the lounge. He carried a stack of rumpled papers piled so high, he couldn't see over the top. There were also scraps of notes rolled up inside his jacket pockets and stuffed into his trousers. His clothing looked as rumpled as the papers he was struggling with.

The old man's curly white hair stuck out in uncombed tufts on either side of his head. As he lifted his chin to peer over the papers, they spilled to the ground. Files, notebooks, computer sheets, and pads scattered across the carpet. "Oh, my goodness," he moaned in a thick foreign accent, "I have made such a mess for certain. Always I make such a mess."

"I'll help you pick it up," said Barney, feeling sorry for him.

The old man slid his bifocals down his nose. "Who is this to whom I'm talking?"

"I'm Barney Prescott," he explained, gathering up the papers.

Glancing down at the mess, the old man seemed unable to cope with it. "Goodness, I have made such a muchly mess. Always I never look to where I am going."

Carefully stacking the piles together, Barney

handed them back, but the old man dropped them all again. "I think you're carrying too much," Barney said. "Let me take some."

"No," he protested, pushing Barney away. "No one must look at my research. No one must steal my secrets. Too many secrets have been stolen. *Dangerous* secrets—all stolen."

"I won't steal anything," Barney assured him. "My parents taught me I should never steal."

The old man looked confused. "Who are your parents? Do I know them?"

"No, I don't think so."

"Then why speak of them?" he asked angrily. "Why confuse me? Too many things they confuse me."

Cassie wondered if the old man was crazy or just eccentric. He was certainly clumsy! "Here, let me help," she offered.

Together, she and Barney got everything picked up and back into the old man's arms. "You're all set now," she said.

The old man stared at her. "Do I know you? What is your name?"

"Cassie Hastings."

The old man looked more confused than ever.

Barney tried to clarify things. "We're here with our great-aunt Alex."

"And who is *she*?"

Cassie explained. "Alexandra Ludlington is a major stockholder in Clarion Pictures."

Hearing this, the old man dropped everything again. "Providence has sent you!" he shouted. He grabbed Barney with one arm and Cassie with the other. "You must come with me. It's a matter of life and death."

"What are you talking about?" asked Barney, trying to push him away.

The old man, remarkably strong, held on to both of them tightly. "Many are in danger," he insisted. "If something is not done quickly, many lives will be lost!"

Chapter Five

"WHERE ARE YOU TAKING US?" ASKED CASSIE AS THE old man dragged them down the corridor.

"You must come to my office," he insisted. "There I have information you must see. Yes, information Mrs. Ludlington must know about."

"Who are you? Do you know Aunt Alex?" asked Barney.

"Hurry," the old man pleaded, "there is so little time." He stopped at the end of the corridor outside an office with the name *Victor Ratoff* written on the door.

"Are you taking us to see Professor Ratoff?" asked Barney.

"*I* am Professor Ratoff," he said, turning a key in the lock. "Come inside quickly," he said, shutting the door behind them.

32

Cassie had never seen such a disorganized mess. There was no place to sit and no light from the windows. Piles of papers were scattered all over and books rose six feet high off the floor. Books were also shoved against the walls, covering the windows. Even the chairs were covered with books, teetering on top of each other about to collapse. "This place looks like a rat's nest," she said, beginning to sneeze.

"Yes, it is a muchly mess," the professor agreed. "But my research must continue. There is so little time left."

"Why'd you bring us here?" asked Barney. "What do you want?"

"Your aunt must insist this studio be shut down," said the professor. "Yes, this must be done at once."

"She won't do that," said Barney. "Aunt Alex won't put people out of work."

"To be out of work is serious, yes," he agreed, "but to be in great danger is more so. Right now, everyone here is in great danger. Each day, it gets stronger. Someday soon, it will surely overtake us."

"It? What's *it*?" asked Barney.

Professor Ratoff started pacing back and forth, nervously fingering his curly tufts of hair. "*It* is causing all the trouble. *It* has a life of its own

33

now. I warned them, no one can say I didn't! But no one would listen to me."

Cassie inched toward the door. "We'd better go now. It's been *très, très charmant* but we must dash."

Professor Ratoff grabbed her arm. "You can't go. I must explain. You must convince your aunt to believe me."

"What are you talking about?" she asked.

"I'm so afraid about this movie," the professor explained. "Never should I have agreed to it, *never*."

"Do you know something about the trouble on *The Monster Master* set?" asked Barney. "People say it's jinxed; do you think so, too?"

"No, it is *cursed*," he replied. "Cursed by a dreadful thing. And it is all my fault. I never meant this to happen but I am to blame."

"Cursed by what?" asked Barney.

"By *it!*" the professor shouted. "*It* is alive and will soon come to get us all."

Barney assumed the professor was crazy.

"You don't believe me, do you?" he asked, sighing. "No one believes me. Everyone laughs and thinks I am not right in the head. But I have *proof*." He began rummaging through the papers on his desk. "All my proof is in here somewhere. All the theories in my book are *true*." With insane energy, Professor Ratoff leafed through books, then quickly threw them aside. "Where are all my notes? I am so absentminded, everything has been stolen from under my nose. You will not believe unless I show you my secrets."

"What secrets?" asked Barney.

The professor's eyes burned with intensity. "Ancient secrets. This information took a lifetime to acquire. Over years, I have unearthed many truths buried beneath myth and legend. The mud creature was said to be myth but I have proved it is real. Oh, yes, my research has proved that absolutely true."

"What's a mud creature?" asked Barney.

Professor Ratoff grabbed Barney's shirt. "Did you know the magicians of ancient Egypt could take dust from under their feet and create creatures to do their will? Oh, yes, with the proper magic words, unbelievable things can be done. But in the wrong hands, unbelievable destruction can be unleashed!"

By now, Cassie was sure the professor was bonkers. She hurried for the door, and was startled to find it was locked. "Let us out of here," she insisted.

"No," said the professor, "you must not go. Are you frightened? I mean no harm. I have information that you must relay to your aunt. This studio must be shut down immediately. The golem creature has inhuman strength but it cannot think for itself. If it becomes the slave of someone evil, it can do great damage."

Barney suddenly felt sorry for the professor. He watched him scurry around his office, searching for his misplaced secrets. "What should we do about this guy?" he whispered to Cassie.

"I guess we'll have to humor him," she answered.

"Don't you believe me?" the professor pleaded.

"Sure we do," said Barney. "Sure, we'll tell our aunt about it. We'll tell her you think there's a mud creature loose around here."

"It is a *golem*," the professor explained. "I wrote about such a creature in my book. When Clarion Pictures bought the rights, I warned them not to experiment with my theories. But they ignored me. Against my wishes, they built such a creature in their laboratory. At first, it couldn't come to life without the secret words—but someone stole my ancient incantations. Someone breathed life into the creature!"

"You think someone brought the mud creature *to life*?" asked Cassie.

"Yes, but the golem was very clever. It *escaped*. Now it is hiding somewhere on the soundstage. Each day it grows stronger. Very soon, no one will be safe from it."

Cassie continued to humor the old man. "No kidding, how could such a thing happen?"

"*Greed*," the professor explained. "If it were not for greed, the creature would never have been created. No one must profit from the ancient secrets. There is danger hidden within the ancient knowledge. I warned them but no one listened. Clarion Pictures wanted to make a fortune scaring people. Instead, they have made a *monster*."

Cassie nervously eyed the door. Someone began banging outside. "Ratoff, are you in there?" a voice shouted out. The professor hurried to unlock it.

David Douglas stood outside, looking furious. "Oliver Crenshaw has been searching for these children," he said angrily. "What are they doing in here?"

"We are having a charming chat," said the professor, quite innocently. "The children are interested in my research."

As Cassie and Barney hurried away, the old man grabbed them back. "Promise you'll tell your aunt everything I said."

"Sure I will," said Barney, "I promise."

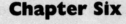

Chapter Six

"IT'S ONE O'CLOCK," SAID CRENSHAW IMPATIENTLY, glancing around the commissary. "Where's your aunt Alex?"

"I guess she's late," said Barney.

"No, Alex is never late; something must've happened. Haven't you noticed how *strangely* she's been acting?"

"Speaking of strange," said Barney, "we spoke to Professor Ratoff and he had something *very* strange to tell us."

"Don't repeat that gibberish," said Cassie.

"I promised."

Crenshaw spied an empty table. "I'm really starved after that meeting. Clarion Pictures is in a bigger mess than I supposed. I can't imagine what's gone wrong here."

"Professor Ratoff says he knows," Barney explained. "He says Clarion Pictures is cursed by a monster."

"A *what*?"

Cassie poked Barney. "Tell him later, I'm hungry, too."

As they sat down, Barney glanced around, hoping to snatch a glimpse of movie stars. "So far, I've seen nobody. Where are all the celebrities?"

"Only bit players eat in the commissary," Cassie explained. "Big stars eat lunch in their private trailers."

As the waitress approached their table, Barney read down the luncheon list. "I'll have the Stallone Baloney Sandwich."

The waitress nodded approvingly. "That tastes great with Matt Dillon Pickles on the side."

"And the Molly Ringwald Jell-O Mold for dessert," he added.

Cassie chose something more glamorous. "I'll have Chicken à la Redford."

"Good choice," said the waitress. "Try it with Paul Newman Dressing."

Crenshaw glanced at the menu. "Dishes with silly names always disguise inferior food. I think I'll have a hamburger."

"What kind? We have a Whoopi Goldberg Whopper Burger or the Cosby Cheeseburger Double Deluxe."

"A *plain* hamburger."

"Suit yourself," said the waitress, gathering up the menus.

"I had quite an informative meeting," Crenshaw confided. "I learned there've been over a dozen accidents on *The Monster Master* set. That's why the picture is so overbudget, but no one can explain the accidents."

"Professor Ratoff says they aren't accidents," said Barney. "It's a *curse*. He says the special effects department built a mud creature that's on the loose."

"Yes, he says there's a creature called a golem wandering around," Cassie added.

"Crazy, right?" asked Barney. "There's no such thing, is there?"

"As what?" asked Crenshaw.

"A *golem*," said Barney. "Have *you* ever heard of a golem?"

Crenshaw was proud of the fact he'd been listed in the *Guinness Book* as the country's smartest man. "A golem? Of course I've heard of it."

"Really?" asked Cassie. "What is it?"

"The golem is a famous legendary creature carved from clay or mud."

"That's what the professor told us," said Cassie, "but we didn't believe it."

"Is it evil?" asked Barney.

"Yes and no," said Crenshaw. "The golem had great strength but it couldn't think for itself. In the hands of a good person it could help people gain justice. But in the hands of an evil person it could do great damage. Legend says that life could be breathed into the creature by writing secret words across its forehead."

Barney shuddered. "Secret words? That's what the professor said, too. He told us someone stole his secret words to bring the creature to life. That's why the golem is hanging around here now. The professor warned everyone but no one believes him."

"I'm not surprised," said Crenshaw. "With the professor spreading that wacky story, no wonder everyone is a nervous wreck. Ratoff must be insane!"

Cassie felt relieved. "I'm glad you don't believe him."

"Of course I don't. A clay creature isn't destroying this studio, it's *sabotage*."

"Really?" asked Barney.

Crenshaw nodded. "I'll bet money on it. Someone has a great deal to gain from these accidents. There's a power play going on here. If Clarion

Pictures' stock value lowers, it'd be easy to take over this studio." He glanced at his watch. "Where on earth is Alex? I'm getting worried, there are too many cuckoos around this place. I think I'll look for her in the lobby."

Barney watched as Crenshaw hurried toward the elevators. "What's up? First Aunt Alex gets all nervous and now Crenshaw. Is it Hollywood or what?"

"Maybe so," said Cassie knowingly. "This *is* the romance capital of the world, you know."

"So what?"

"So it's obvious, stupid. We're witnessing a romance. Crenshaw has fallen in love."

"He has? With who?"

"With Aunt Alex, of course."

"Quit kidding."

"Perhaps it's hard to believe but it's definitely an *affaire de cœur*. Look how worried he is about her. Crenshaw can't let Aunt Alex out of his sight. After all these years of working for her, he's fallen in *love*."

"But they're both so *old*," Barney argued.

"Nevertheless."

"No, you're way off base," said Barney. "A smart guy like Crenshaw wouldn't waste his time on mushy junk like that. He's a *businessman*."

"So why did he rush off to search for Aunt Alex?"

"Maybe he wants to *protect* her." Barney glanced at a woman walking toward them. "She looks familiar. Hey, I finally found a celebrity. Isn't she a famous actress?" The woman approaching had fluffy tufts of pale blond hair. She was wearing a bold floral print dress with an oversized hat to match. "You think maybe she's a big soap opera star?"

"What's wrong with you, stupid?" said Cassie. "That's *Aunt Alex*."

Barney blinked and looked again. "Are you sure?"

"Do you like the new me?" asked Aunt Alex eagerly.

"What have you done to yourself?" asked Cassie.

"Can you really notice the difference?"

"Sure we can," said Barney. "How'd it happen?"

Aunt Alex fluffed up her already fluffy hair. "It's called a make-over," she explained, "but this hair color isn't permanent, it'll wash out. I was feeling reckless and—well, it's unusual, don't you think?"

"Yeah, unusual," said Barney. "What happened to your real clothes?"

"Thrown away," she explained. "That's the whole idea behind a make-over: Everything you have is thrown out. It's not such a bad idea. Maybe everyone should throw everything away once in a while, don't you agree?"

"Maybe not *everything*," said Barney. "Couldn't you get some of the old stuff back?"

Aunt Alex glanced down at her new floral print dress. "Don't you like this outfit? I passed so many wonderful shops on Rodeo Drive, I couldn't resist buying something."

"It's very dramatic," said Cassie tactfully.

"But?"

"But are you sure it's *you*, Aunt Alex?"

"No, dear," she admitted, "I'm not at all sure." Aunt Alex pulled up a chair and sat down. "Suddenly I'm not sure of anything."

Crenshaw returned, looking relieved. "Thank goodness you're back, I've been searching everywhere." He stared at Alex's outfit. "Goodness, don't you look—"

"Glamorous?"

"Different."

"Do you think it's *me*?"

"Of course it's you. I've known you for thirty years!"

"Forget I asked," said Aunt Alex, grabbing a menu. "Let's eat."

"The food doesn't look too promising," said Crenshaw. "I'll bet it's like everything else at Clarion Pictures—a disaster. Let's hurry and eat so we can start touring the soundstage. I'm hoping the actors can shed some light on what's going wrong over there."

Aunt Alex dropped her menu. "You're visiting the actors? No, Ollie, I can't tour the soundstage. Not yet—not today—not like this."

"Like what?" asked Crenshaw. "Why not? That was our plan."

"That was *this morning*," she argued, "but this is now and things are all different."

"Alex, you're not making sense," said Crenshaw. "You're not yourself."

"No, I'm not myself today," she agreed, "not the *real* me. In fact," she added, "I'm not even very hungry today. So why am I here?" She pushed her chair aside and stood up. "I'm returning to the hotel. Maybe I'll lie down awhile."

Aunt Alex placed the floppy floral hat on her head then hurried toward the exit.

Cassie and Barney stared after her.

"Are you sure that was our aunt Alex?" asked Barney.

Crenshaw looked concerned. "I've worked for that woman forever and she's never behaved so strangely! *Why* won't she meet with the actors? Why won't she go near the set? What is she trying to avoid?"

Cassie finally saw an opportunity to get the VIP passes. "Why don't we find out?" she suggested. "We'll visit the soundstage ourselves after lunch."

Crenshaw watched the waitress return with their orders. "Lunch? No, thanks, I've lost my appetite."

"Do you really think that set is being *sabotaged*?" asked Barney.

"I'd bank on it," said Crenshaw, pushing aside his hamburger.

Cassie's wheels kept turning. "In that case, you should keep far away from that set. If *you* showed up, someone would get suspicious. Everyone knows you represent a major stockholder; they'd be on their guard."

Crenshaw knew Cassie was driving at something. "What are you suggesting?"

"*I'll* snoop around for you," she offered. "I'll find out what Aunt Alex is trying to avoid and discover who's sabotaging things."

Crenshaw was amused. "Are you volunteering to be a *spy*?"

"No fair," said Barney. "You can't spy without *me*. I'm going, too."

"So I have *two* spies?" Crenshaw considered the offer. "I'd do anything to protect Alex's interests as long as it's *safe*."

"We won't get in any trouble," Barney assured

46

him. "Cassie knows how to be real sneaky. She's the sneakiest person ever."

"No, I don't like it. What if people are right and that set is *jinxed*? Something awful might happen to you both."

"Not to me," said Cassie.

Barney agreed. "Right, Cassie is too mean for anything to happen to her."

"No," said Crenshaw, "the fact remains that lots of things have gone wrong on that set—all of them unexpected."

"Did you *lie* to us?" asked Barney. "Do you believe Professor Ratoff? Do you think a monster is on the loose over there?"

"Don't be silly," Crenshaw protested. "The golem is merely a legend."

"So don't worry," said Cassie. "Get us a VIP pass and let's go."

"Oh, all right," Crenshaw finally agreed, "I'll let you go."

Chapter Seven

"REMEMBER," SAID CRENSHAW, "BE SURE TO SNOOP *discreetly*."

Barney fingered his special VIP badge. "Don't worry, we're on the job."

Cassie grew excited as they walked along the back lot to the soundstage of *The Monster Master* set. At last she'd get to meet celebrities! But as they approached soundstage 26, she noticed a sign outside the metal door: CLOSED SET, KEEP OUT!

"That doesn't mean us, does it?" she asked.

"It means *everybody*," said the guard at the door. "No one gets in without special permission from Harvey Winston, the director."

Cassie and Barney proudly flashed their VIP badges.

"If the head office okayed it, I guess it's okay," said the guard, unlocking the door.

"Remember," said Crenshaw, waving good-bye as the children entered the soundstage, *"discretion."*

Barney winked and nodded. The guard returned to his post, then the heavy metal doors of soundstage 26 slowly closed behind them.

As Barney glanced around, he felt he'd left the real world far behind. He'd entered the dark, cavernous open-sesame world of movie make-believe.

Overhead cameras mounted on specially constructed dolly tracks and cranes were being maneuvered around by cameramen as if they were spaceships. Miles of wire cables snaked along the ground and there was confusion everywhere.

"Let's find Harvey Winston," said Cassie. "It's the director's job to give important guests a personal tour. But remember, we don't want to look like *tourists.*"

Barney tripped over a lump of coiled cable. "Quit telling me that, okay?" He stopped a man who was passing, to ask "Are you Harvey Winston?"

"No, I'm the prop master," he replied.

Another man hurried past them. "Are you Harvey Winston?" Barney asked.

"No, I'm the key grip and I'm in a hurry."

Cassie approached an old man seated in a corner. "Are you the director?"

"No way," said the man, looking up from his clipboard. "Don't bother me, I'm preparing call sheets for tomorrow's shooting."

As Cassie and Barney proceeded, they walked past a set construction that looked like the outside of a Victorian mansion. It was dimly lit by artificial moonlight. While one technician tested the mechanical snow drum, another mounted the rain machine on wire cables. Other crewmen were scattering dry ice and oil-fog machines around the stage floor. "Watch out!" one of them shouted as Barney bumped into him. "This fog juice can be hazardous." Another crewman shouted down from the rigging beside the snow machine, "Clear the set below!"

"I never knew movie-making was so *dangerous*," said Barney.

"Where's Harvey Winston?" asked Cassie impatiently.

Everyone they spoke to steered them to someone else. They asked the construction coordinator, the assistant designer, the gaffer, and the set director. Finally, they spoke to Mitch, the second assistant director, and he told them they couldn't go any farther.

"Look, kids, this is a closed set," Mitch explained. "Get out of the way, we're setting up a shot."

Cassie and Barney backed away as two large cameras on tracking devices were wheeled into place. Hairstylists, secretaries, production assistants, and script supervisors all ran around in wild confusion.

"Everything looks so realistic," Barney observed.

"Hollywood can make anything seem real," said Cassie with admiration.

The set construction, on a split-level platform, reproduced the inside of the mansion. On one side of the soundstage there was a living room and on the other, a formal dining room. Below this lay a dark, moldy basement covered in cobwebs. Inside the basement, two propmen were busy repairing the artificial spiderwebs that had loosened from the fiberglass stone wall. Nearby, an animal trainer waited with a cageful of trained rats that were scheduled to skitter across the set on cue.

Cassie cringed when she saw the rats. "How disgusting."

"No, they're cute," said Barney. "I read they cover actors with peanut butter to get rats to crawl over them. You think that's true?"

Mitch came running toward them. "I told you kids to keep away from here."

"We're *VIP's,*" Cassie insisted.

"Who cares?" he shouted, gesturing them into

a corner. Then he turned toward the crew. "Okay, everyone, quiet on the set, Angela Marley is coming!"

Cassie was delighted. "*Angela Marley!* Is *she* in this picture?"

Mitch nodded. "Yes, she's our female lead. And she's an hour late, as usual."

Cassie couldn't believe her good fortune. Angela Marley was her all-time favorite movie star. To Cassie, she was more than just a star, she was a symbol. When Cassie was being bounced around from one boarding school to another, going to movies was her only link with home. And seeing Angela Marley movies made her feel connected to something. "Angela Marley is magnificent!" she said.

"Oh, yeah?" asked Barney. "What kind of movies does she make?"

Cassie recalled all the nights she'd cried herself to sleep in foreign boarding schools. Watching Angela Marley movies had always made her smile again. "She makes *wonderful* movies and I've seen every one of them."

After a few minutes, Angela Marley made her dramatic entrance onto the set. She was accompanied by two hairstylists, a wardrobe mistress, a makeup artist, and a press agent. "Where's Harvey Winston?" she asked. "I can't possibly be directed by an *assistant*." Angela ran her fingers through her platinum blond hair as the wardrobe mistress adjusted the folds of her pale blue robe.

"Doesn't she look beautiful?" asked Cassie.

"I think she looks snooty," said Barney. "No wonder *you* like her."

At last Harvey Winston appeared. He was tall and thin and rushed onto the set, out of breath. "I was up in the editing room. So far, we've edited and scored over three hundred thousand feet of flim and two hundred thousand have been printed. But we have almost *nothing* we can use. It's a nightmare!"

"This robe doesn't work for me, Harvey," said Angela. "The color is all wrong."

"You already *approved* the wardrobe, Angela."

"I didn't approve this *color*," she argued. "It's not appropriate, Harv, you'll have to change it."

"*What?*" asked Harvey Winston, growing furious.

"You heard me. And I think there should more scrim shots in my scenes. I watched my rushes this morning and the audience can't see my *face*."

"Who do you think you are anyway?" Winston shouted.

Angela Marley looked shocked. "I'm the star of this movie, naturally."

"*You're* not the star," he argued. "That big machine from SP-EFX is the real star of *The Monster*

Master." Harvey Winston shouted to the lighting engineer, "Move that scoop in here!" and the crewmen moved a wide-angle floodlight closer.

"That big ugly machine isn't a *person*," Angela argued. "People are the true stars of movies."

"No, they're not," he shouted, "not since the good old days when we made real movies with real dialogue and real actresses!"

"Take that back," Angela shouted. "And will you change this robe or not?"

"Absolutely not," said Harvey Winston firmly.

"Then I refuse to work," she replied. "I'm too upset to begin the scene."

"Don't you dare walk off this set again," he ordered. "You've done that three times already this week. What's up, Angela? Are you trying to *destroy* Clarion Pictures? I heard you bought stock in a rival company. I'll bet you're trying to sabotage this movie!"

Barney nudged Cassie. "Hey, Crenshaw was right!" He fumbled in his pocket for his pad and pencil. "Maybe we solved the mystery. I'd better take notes."

Cassie wasn't listening. It broke her heart to see Angela Marley so upset. She *hated* Harvey Winston for being so mean to her.

Tension mounted on the set.

"If that's the way you feel," said Angela dramatically, then she stormed off with her entourage trailing behind her.

The cameraman groaned, the boom man grumbled, and the script girl threw her papers into the air.

Harvey Winston did a slow burn as he threw himself into his canvas chair. "Relight the set for Basil Trelawny," he shouted. "Sometimes I think I'd *sell my soul* to find an actor who'll take direction!"

"Are you kids still hanging around here?" asked Mitch. "You'd better stand clear. Winston needs time to cool off or he'll blow his stack."

"No, I can't go," Cassie protested. "I've got to meet Angela Marley."

"We came to meet the stars," Barney explained. "We're VIP's."

Mitch scratched his head. "You want VIP treatment? Come with me and I'll show you the *real* star of this movie."

Chapter Eight

"THERE IT IS," SAID MITCH PROUDLY, "OUR MIRACLE of modern technology."

"What is it?" asked Barney.

"We call it The Clump."

Mitch had led the children toward the end of the soundstage behind the mansion set. Things were alive with activity as the movie's mechanical monster was being prepared for a shot. Various pieces of The Clump were scattered around being worked on by the crew. Three people were repairing a crack in The Clump's mechanical head. In the rear, The Clump's legs were being painted. The Clump's hands were lying on the ground as three workmen oiled the inside mechanism.

"It's awfully big," said Barney.

"Yes, in the script The Clump keeps growing. This big one is twenty feet high and we've nicknamed it Clump Three. In the scenes where the monster is normal size, an actor portrays the role. We call him Clump Two. We also had another monster we called Clump One but we ditched it."

"Why?" asked Cassie.

"It was a big dud," Mitch explained. "The SP-EFX Department first tried making a monster from real clay."

"Just like Professor Ratoff wrote about in his book?" asked Cassie.

Mitch nodded. "The crew dug up pounds of red clay from behind the back lot. But it weighed a ton and the special effects guys couldn't install their machinery in it properly. It turned out so badly, they scrapped the entire mess. But this one has problems, too," Mitch admitted. "It's always breaking down mysteriously. Frankly, I think someone is short-circuiting the apparatus."

"Do you suspect *sabotage*?" asked Barney.

"Maybe so. Actors don't like machines. There's an old saying, never work with kids or animals. I'd include machines, too. Actors are *jealous* of them. Machines steal work away from actors and sometimes, they steal *scenes*, too."

"That's silly," said Cassie. "An oily machine can't replace a movie star."

"Very interesting," said Barney, writing everything down.

"Quiet on the set!" a voice shouted out.

"I've got to get back now," Mitch explained as he hurried away. "I think Basil Trelawny is starting his scene."

Cassie and Barney quickly followed and arrived back on the dressed set in time to see Basil Trelawny make his entrance.

The old actor was impeccably dressed. A long black cape lay draped over his shoulders and his gray hair surrounded an angular, sensitive face. He glanced at the ground to find his chalk mark. Then he waited as the lighting engineer adjusted the exposure meter and the boom man took a sound reading.

"He looks so distinguished," said Cassie.

"He was once known as the Great Face," Mitch explained. "Gordon Douglas found him on Broadway, brought him to Hollywood, and made him a movie star. In the old days, Trelawny got thousands of fan letters each week. I suppose all his fans are dead now. It's sad when the old ones come out of retirement. I guess he's penniless. They say Gordon Douglas cheated Trelawny out of a fortune."

"You mean G.D., the Terror of Tinseltown, was also a *cheat*?" Barney took more notes. "Hey, maybe we've got *two* suspects, Cassie. Which one do you think is sabotaging this place?"

Cassie wasn't listening. She was watching Basil Trelawny as he began to speak.

"Mr. Winston, if you are prepared to roll the cameras, I am prepared to begin my scene."

Harvey Winston jumped from his chair and shouted to his cameraman, "Let's use a fish-eye lens on this shot." Then he approached the old actor. "Okay, Trelawny, this is the pivotal scene in the movie. The audience is waiting for you to bring The Clump to life, see? They're hanging on to the edge of their seats. So far, there's been no blood or guts in this film and they're getting hungry for it, see? They hope you discover the secret words to bring the monster to life, see?"

Basil Trelawny looked indignant. "No, I don't see. I disagree with your interpretation, Mr. Winston. You're directing this film as if it were a *horror* movie."

"It *is*."

"Nonsense! I don't work in horror movies. They're beneath my dignity."

"Stop living in the Dark Ages. No one makes *your* kind of movies anymore. People don't care about *plots*."

"Yes, Hollywood has changed," said Basil Trelawny sadly, "but I refuse to play second fiddle to a *machine.* I also refuse to work on a set where I'm being *spied* upon."

"Quit joking," Winston argued. "No one's spying on you."

"I'm *watched* every day," Basil Trelawny insisted, pointing toward the corners of the set. "Someone is hiding *there* and *there*—and *there.*"

"Who?" asked Harvey Winston.

"Whoever it is never shows himself but he's *watching.* I can feel his presence breathing down my back!"

"You're nuts!" Harvey Winston shouted. "Let's start this scene. The day's almost over and I don't have a decent foot of film."

Basil Trelawny stepped off his chalk mark. "That's because you've no idea what this film is about. An actor needs *motivation* and it's your job to provide it."

"And it's your job to *act,*" Winston argued. "Getting a paycheck is your motivation."

"I refuse to be spoken to that way," said Trelawny, turning away. "When you've apologized, I'll continue."

"Fat chance!" Winston shouted as he watched Trelawny hurry off the set.

Mitch shook his head. "Harvey Winston can't get along with actors."

"What's his problem?" asked Cassie.

"A terrible temper," Mitch explained, "and Winston hates everyone. He even hates this studio."

"Why?" asked Barney.

"Years ago, Gordon Douglas destroyed Harvey's father's career. Harvey never forgave him and he never forgot."

"What a mess," said Barney, busily writing. "*Everyone* has a grudge against Clarion Pictures!"

As the crew began to relight the mansion set for another shot, Cassie heard a creaking noise from overhead. She looked up toward the large structure high above the soundstage. There, an air shaft made of wood had been painted to look like metal. It hung suspended on heavy chains from the ceiling. Supported by an iron brace, it was broad enough to hold a large camera.

Cassie gasped as she saw the huge structure begin to sway from side to side. The camera resting on top began to slide back and forth precariously. Then it teetered along the scaffolding, poised to fall to the ground.

Suddenly, Cassie saw a strange blobby shape emerge from behind the camera. It was *huge*. It was a large reddish-brownish lumpy thing with two arms, two legs, two piercing eyes, and an insane grin.

Cassie couldn't believe it. As she screamed out a warning, the horrid creature became frightened by the sound. It pushed the camera off the scaffolding, sending it hurtling in Cassie's direction!

Chapter Nine

"DID YOU SEE IT?" ASKED CASSIE. "DID YOU SEE THAT big ugly thing crawling around up there? Where'd it go? Did it get away?"

With split-second timing, Mitch had pushed Cassie aside just before the camera came crashing down. It now lay in pieces by her feet, ruined beyond repair.

"What a colossal mess!" shouted Harvey Winston. "Who's responsible for this? What happened? Where'd these *kids* comes from?"

Cassie stared up at the scaffolding. The creature had disappeared. "It must've escaped!"

"What'd you see up there?" asked Barney.

"I think it was a *monster*. It was a big blobby thing and it tried to kill me!"

63

Harvey Winston scratched his head. "Who's this crazy kid? Get her out of here."

"Go see if that blob is still up there," Cassie insisted.

No one moved.

"Don't you *believe* me?" Cassie asked.

The cameramen, boom men, and engineers all shook their heads and shrugged. No one else had seen anything, not even Barney.

"Who are these two troublemakers?" asked Harvey Winston.

"They're VIP's," Mitch explained. "These kids are relatives of Mrs. Ludlington, a major stockholder."

"That's different," said Winston, backing off. He gestured to his crew. "Someone check that scaffolding and see what's up there."

Both the gaffer and the key grip volunteered. They tried scaling the tall ladder beside the construction but a crane camera obstructed the way.

"Move that whirly," Harvey Winston shouted.

The head cameraman crawled over the base of the crane, then climbed onto the seat to maneuver the camera away from the scaffolding. Cautiously, the two crewmen walked the plank until they'd reached the end of the simulated air shaft.

"Hey, that kid is right," the key grip shouted down, "there *is* someone up here."

"Is it a monster?" asked Winston jokingly.

The gaffer scratched his head. "Yeah, I suppose so. It's Fred Fisher, the actor who plays The Clump."

"Fisher? What's *he* doing up there?"

"Search me," shouted the key grip, "but he doesn't look too hot. I think he's unconscious."

Winston got furious. *"Drunk?* I warned Fisher about drinking on the job. Bring him down at once."

Together, the crew members carried the actor across the scaffolding and down the ladder, then laid him on the ground.

Harvey Winston looked down at the man. "Well, kids, there's your mysterious creature—a drunken actor in a monster suit."

Cassie stared at the man in The Clump suit. The creature she'd seen was five times bigger and scarier-looking. "No, this isn't him."

Suddenly, Mitch interrupted. "Hey, Fred isn't drunk, there's something wrong with him. Let's check his air hose." Mitch pulled off Fisher's monster head. "Just as I thought. Fred's air tube ripped out of his mouth. Another few minutes inside this costume and he would've suffocated."

"What a horrible death," said Barney. "Snuffed out inside a Clump costume!"

Once Fisher's latex headpiece was removed, he began panting for breath. "I thought I was a goner," he gasped.

"What were you doing up there?" asked Harvey Winston.

Fred Fisher sucked in several deep breaths. "I was *dragged* up. A huge creature sneaked up behind me and knocked me out. It must've ripped out my air hose, then dumped me on the scaffolding."

"A likely story," shouted Winston. "Admit it, Fisher, you were *drunk*."

"I wasn't drunk," Fisher insisted, "I was attacked. I arrived on the set early and before I knew it, a big blob came out of nowhere!" He removed the monster suit and threw it to the ground. "Too many strange things have happened here. It's not safe working on this creepy set. I *quit*."

"You can't quit," Winston shouted, "you're *fired*. And the price of that camera comes out of your salary."

"I'm *suing* Clarion Pictures," Fred Fisher protested. "I'm calling my agent. Being attacked by a creature isn't in my contract!" Then he stormed off the set.

Harvey Winston threw himself into his chair. "Only a nut would believe a story like that!"

Cassie believed it.

It was a crazy story, but she believed it.

Cassie knew the creature who'd hurled the camera to the ground wasn't Fred Fisher in a monster suit.

It was a *real* monster, just as Professor Ratoff had warned.

It was the dreaded golem. Cassie had *seen* it!

Chapter Ten

CASSIE STARED AT BARNEY AS HE SAT ON THE BED WITH a wicker tray on his lap. "This trip has turned you into a greedy little pig! How can you eat all those appetizers before dinner?"

Barney took a bite of beluga caviar. "Aunt Alex said I could taste everything in the hotel." He spit it out. "Yucchh, salty slime." He tasted the artichoke hearts vinaigrette. "This stinks, too."

Cassie pushed his tray aside. "Stop being childish. C'mon, let's figure out what to do about the *monster*. If no one captures it, that creature might hide on the soundstage forever."

Barney laughed. "There's no monster, stupid."

"Of course there is."

"You've seen too many horror movies. Be logical, Cassie. You said Fred Fisher wasn't the monster, right?"

"Right."

"And the Clump machine wasn't the monster either, right?"

"Right."

"So there *is* no monster. That's simple logic, right?"

"Wrong. There's got to be a monster because I *saw* it. And Fred Fisher saw it, too," Cassie reminded him.

"He was drunk," Barney protested. "No, the accidents on that set are sabotage, just like Crenshaw suspected. Everyone hates Clarion Pictures and one of them is trying to ruin the studio. Luckily, I've figured out which one," he added proudly. "It's Angela Marley, that snooty actress you're so nuts about." Barney brushed some crumbs from his shirt and strolled across the room. "She's the one who's put the whammy on this picture."

"Don't say a word against Angela," Cassie shouted angrily. "Angela would never do a thing like that, *never*."

"Sure she would," said Barney, realizing he'd hit a nerve. "Angela Marley owns stock in a rival company so she wants Clarion Pictures to go bust. You saw how she tried to foul up the production."

Cassie would rather have died than believe anything bad about Angela Marley. "If it's sabotage, someone else is responsible. What about Basil Trelawny? He gets my vote. He hates the movie he's in and he hates the director, too."

Before Barney could argue the point, Crenshaw rushed into the room. "Good, you kids are back; I was getting worried."

"Hey, thanks for the limo ride," said Barney. "It was great finding the chauffeur waiting for us."

"What did you learn?" asked Crenshaw impatiently. "Alex will be coming by soon to pick us up for dinner, so fill me in fast. What's Alex afraid of on that movie set? What's she avoiding over there?"

"I don't know," Barney admitted, "but I learned who's responsible for the sabotage. It's—"

"Don't you dare repeat those lies," Cassie screamed, then threw a pillow into Barney's face.

Barney threw it back. "They're not lies," he insisted. "Snooty Angela Marley is to blame for everything."

"You're crazy!" Cassie shouted. "If the monster isn't to blame, then it's Basil Trelawny. Angela has too much class to do such a tacky thing."

Suddenly, Aunt Alex entered the room. "What's going on here? It looks an awful lot like a pillow fight."

Cassie and Barney stopped to stare at Aunt Alex. Barney noticed she made a funny squishy sound as she walked. "What're you wearing, Aunt A.?"

"These are called crinolines," she explained. As Aunt Alex swirled around the room, the net petticoats underneath her skirt began to rustle. "They were popular thirty-five years ago and now they've come back into style. Do you think they're too youthful for me?"

"Why keep changing yourself around?" asked Barney.

"Are you still searching for the real you?" asked Cassie.

"Perhaps I am," Aunt Alex admitted, "but I'm having trouble *finding* it."

"Well, that isn't it," said Barney frankly. "You should wear your big lumpy sweater instead. You look real cuddly in your big lumpy sweater."

Aunt Alex glanced at herself in the mirror. "No, I don't want to look cuddly. I want to look . . ." She sighed. "Oh, never mind. What's the reason for the pillow fight?"

"Barney was telling disgusting *lies*," said Cassie.

"No, I wasn't!"

"It seems the children disagree as to who is sabotaging the movie set. Cassie feels that Basil

71

Trelawny may be responsible for the trouble, but Barney disagrees."

"What are you talking about?" asked Aunt Alex.

"Crenshaw sent us over to the movie set to spy on people," Barney explained. "He was absolutely right, too. There's dirty business going on over there."

Aunt Alex looked stunned. "*Spying?* You sent the children to spy, Ollie? How dare you do such a thing?"

Crenshaw turned red. "No, it's not the way it sounds, Alex."

"Well, it sounds dreadful! You're supposed to be tutoring the children—giving them knowledge. Instead, I find you're teaching them to spy!"

"I did it for you, Alex. I'm trying to protect your interests. That's why I need to find out the facts."

"That's no excuse," Aunt Alex scolded. "Shame on you, Ollie—defiling the name of a great actor by suggesting he's involved in sabotage."

"You mean Basil Trelawny?" asked Crenshaw. "No, *I* didn't say anything bad about him. I was only repeating—"

"Repeating what?" snapped Aunt Alex. "Idle gossip? No, Ollie, I refuse to listen. Basil Trelawny was the finest Shakespearean actor of his day. When he came out to Hollywood, the stage lost a great performer—and *I* lost—well, never mind about that."

"You *know* him, I *knew* it!" said Crenshaw excitedly. "Is that why you refused to go onto the soundstage? Why are you avoiding Basil Trelawny?"

Aunt Alex blushed. "That's none of your business, Ollie. Just promise me you won't allow the children to spy on him or anyone else."

As Cassie listened, she noticed how fiercely Aunt Alex defended Basil Trelawny—just as fiercely as Cassie had defended Angela Marley. *Why?*

"I'm getting awfully hungry," said Barney. "Let's eat."

"No, I want Ollie's promise first," said Aunt Alex.

Crenshaw sighed deeply. "You know I'd promise you *anything*, Alex." He put his arm around her shoulder. "Now let's go to dinner and forget this whole affair."

"That's it," Cassie whispered. "I've solved the puzzle. I know why Aunt Alex is acting so strangely."

"Then fill me in," said Barney.

"This may not be a simple *affaire de cœur*," Cassie explained. "Perhaps it's a *ménage à trois*."

"Huh? What's that?"

"Shhh," said Cassie, following Aunt Alex out of the room. "I'll explain it to you after dinner."

73

*   *   *

Barney wouldn't believe it. "That old guy Basil Trelawny? You think Aunt Al is *in love* with him?"

Cassie and Barney were seated on lounge chairs beside the empty pool. The sun had just gone down and the lights from the hotel windows were slowly being switched on.

"It's obvious," said Cassie. "Aunt Alex has probably loved him from afar for years. In fact, I'll bet she's his only living fan."

"And I'll bet you're nuts," said Barney. "What's with you? First you say Crenshaw loves Aunt Alex. Now you say Aunt Alex loves Basil Trelawny."

"Yes, affairs of the heart can be complicated."

"But they're all so *old*."

"No one's too old if they're young at heart," said Cassie dramatically.

"Where do you get this stuff?" asked Barney.

"Feminine intuition."

"Feminine intuition told you Crenshaw loves Aunt A.?"

"That's right."

"And it told you Aunt A. loves Basil Trelawny?"

"Uh-huh."

"Then feminine intuition is garbage," said Barney. As he sat in silence staring toward the pool, he suddenly had second thoughts. What if Cassie was right? If she was right about the silly romance

74

stuff, she might also be right about what happened on the set. "Did you *really* see a monster on that scaffolding?" he asked.

"I swear it," said Cassie, "so stop trying to blame Angela Marley for everything. Face it, Professor Ratoff was right—there's a monster on the loose."

"But where did it come from? If it's not the Clump machine or the actor playing The Clump, then what is it?"

"It's the *original* Clump," said Cassie. "I just remembered what Mitch told us. He said the special effects department made a monster from *real clay.*"

"That's right," Barney agreed. "He said they built it just like the one in the legend was built. And then they got rid of it. But how? Where do you suppose they dumped The Clump?"

"I don't know," said Cassie, "but I think we'd better find out."

Barney stared out the window of the stretch limousine. "Are you sure we should do this?" he asked apprehensively.

"Don't be such a wimp," Cassie scolded. "Aunt Alex put the limo at our disposal and the chauffeur has orders to take us wherever we like."

"But I haven't had breakfast yet," he grumbled. "I can't search for a Clump on an empty stomach."

"Forget about food. The sooner we find The Clump, the sooner you'll drop your idiotic theory about Angela Marley."

"Where should we look first?" he asked.

"That's simple, we'll return to the scene of the crime. We'll go to the place where The Clump was born!"

Chapter Eleven

THE SPECIAL EFFECTS LAB COVERED AN ENTIRE FLOOR of an adjoining building on the back lot. When Cassie and Barney flashed their VIP badges, the guard ushered them into the lobby. As they walked down the long, empty corridor, every door bore the ominous message KEEP OUT.

"Why is everything so secretive?" Barney asked. "I wonder what goes on inside those lab rooms."

"It's very suspicious," Cassie agreed. She approached a door and turned the knob. It was locked. She tried several other doors . . . all locked. "What's everyone hiding?"

Barney saw a door marked FOAM FACTORY. "Look, this one is open," he said, turning the knob.

As he and Cassie entered, they noticed foul-smelling liquids resting on a row of electric stoves. They saw a huge walk-in oven against one wall with slabs of foam rubber piled beside it. There was also a structure resembling a giant phone booth with colored spray paints splattered against its walls. In the next room, tools and implements lay scattered on tables.

"What a creepy place," Barney observed. "Like Frankenstein's laboratory. You suppose this is where the clay monster was created?" Behind the lab table there hung a heavy white drapery. "What's back there?" he asked, pulling it open.

Cassie screamed. Lying on the cot behind the curtain she saw a disgustingly gory sight. It was the severed head of a man, its dead eyes staring blankly into space. Blood dripped from its neck and oozed along the floor.

Barney felt he was about to faint.

Cassie screamed again, then ran. As she reached the door, a large hand emerged and grabbed her. "Realistic, isn't it?"

Cassie turned around. A tall fat man with horn-rimmed glasses and long stringy hair stood grinning down at her. "I'm so glad you're frightened. That means my new creation is a success. I'm Adam Demetrius and I run this department. My new blood tubes work well, don't you think? Look how they ooze all over. Loathsome, isn't it?"

"I knew that thing wasn't real," Barney pretended, "but girls always get carried away."

Mr. Demetrius unhooked the tubes invisibly attached to the severed head. He picked it up and cradled it in his arms. "It's amazing what a person can do with fiberglass and latex these days." He extended the head toward Cassie. "See, it's a life mask. The blood is from a wonderful new recipe I've concocted. I take Karo syrup, red dye, paraben, and a few other secret ingredients. Quite effective, isn't it?"

"Quite disgusting," said Cassie, pushing it away.

"Perhaps you'd like to see some of my other creations?" Mr. Demetrius offered. "They're all made with my special formulas. I'm working on several secret projects I can't reveal, but someday mechanical creations will be almost human." He chuckled to himself, then hurried to the closet and removed several sacks of slimy, oozy material. "These are my artificial entrails. We use pounds of them in splatter movies."

"This guy even *sounds* like Frankenstein," Barney mumbled.

Adam Demetrius was thrilled with his own creations. "Oh, let me show you my new gelatin eye plugs, too." He ran back to the closet. "I've made lots of false eyeballs for *The Monster Master*. There's a scene where The Clump rips someone's face off.

79

He pulls off scalps, too, so I've prepared lots of mortician's wax. And lots of bloody body parts." He laughed again. "Theater owners may have to pass out barf bags in the lobby for this movie."

Cassie looked queasy. Adam Demetrius looked delighted. "Disgusted? Wonderful. If I can make you sick, my work has been successful. I wish I had more disgusting things to show you."

"Show us The Clump," said Barney. "I hear you made the original one for the movie."

"That wasn't a success, it was a failure," said Adam Demetrius. "I spent weeks on that thing. I gave it radio-controlled, automated eyes. I constructed splints inside the clay molds to make it walk. Then I placed compressed air vents inside its body for more mobility. That Clump had my most sophisticated equipment but it just wouldn't work."

"What did you do with it?" asked Cassie.

"I dumped that Clump," he said disgustedly. "It's in the storage vault. We keep lots of things in there in hopes we can use them elsewhere."

"Can we see it?" asked Cassie.

"Why? What for?"

"Because we think your work is *fascinating*," she replied slyly.

Adam Demetrius was flattered. "All right, I'll

show you The Clump." He led them through the lab and down the hall.

"What goes on in all those locked rooms?" asked Barney.

"Never mind. They're top-secret projects so don't ask."

The storage vault was a huge room at the end of the corridor. "This place is more precious than a bank vault," Mr. Demetrius explained. "Special effects cost a fortune so we always try to recycle them." He pushed open the heavy metal door.

Cassie stared into the cavernous semidarkness. Bizarre collections of things rested in every corner. She saw severed body parts, a giant latex rat, and a set of large plastic hairy legs.

"This place is filled with strange stuff," said Barney. "How'll we find The Clump?"

Adam Demetrius hurried down the aisle. "We dumped him down at that end. Don't worry, we can't miss him, he's ten feet high!"

Cassie and Barney checked through the aisle. They saw miniature flying saucers, robot costumes, models of the *Titanic* and the Eiffel Tower. They saw lizardmen outfits, a giant tongue, and mechanical man-eating plants. But they didn't see The Clump.

"Nope, he's not here," said Barney.

"He's got to be somewhere," Mr. Demetrius insisted.

After a careful examination of the vault, The Clump couldn't be found.

"It's impossible," said Adam Demetrius. "Where'd it go? After all, it couldn't get up and walk away!"

"Are you sure it was in here?" Cassie asked.

"Of course I'm sure, I saw it. I was very upset when The Clump didn't work, so my staff threw me a party to cheer me up. We all came in here for champagne and cake after we'd dumped The Clump. For a joke, someone suggested we read Professor Ratoff's words over the thing."

"Did you do it?" Cassie asked.

"Sure, it was only a joke but we said some words."

"Where'd you get the words?" Barney asked.

"We sneaked into the professor's office and took some research papers from his desk. Ratoff has hundreds of spells written down, so we picked a few and said the words aloud over The Clump. Then we drank our champagne, had a good laugh, locked the vault, and went back to work." Mr. Demetrius scratched his head as he glanced around. "And now that stupid thing has disappeared. Go figure it."

"I think it escaped," Cassie said.

"It what?"

"She thinks it escaped," Barney reiterated. "Cassie says The Clump is prowling around, doing evil things."

"Maybe you're a better special effects expert than you realize," she suggested. "Maybe those secret words breathed life into The Clump."

"And now it's destroying this place," Barney added.

"Destruction? Impossible! If that was true, I could be *sued*. I mean, I'm not responsible for anything, don't blame me."

"If The Clump is on the loose, it could be hiding anywhere," Barney said. He hurried toward the exit of the vault. "Maybe we should check all the lab rooms."

"No, you can't go in those rooms," Mr. Demetrius protested. "I experiment with explosive devices in there."

"It's important we search everywhere," Cassie told him.

"No, I've got secret equipment," he shouted. "If rival studios find out what I'm doing, they'll steal my inventions." Suddenly, Mr. Demetrius grew suspicious. "What's going on, have you kids deceived me? Pulling my leg, are you? What do you really want here, my *secrets*? You kids are actually *spies*, aren't you?"

"Maybe we are spies," Barney admitted. "I mean we *were* spies, but—"

"I knew it!" he shouted. "This nonsense about The Clump was meant to distract me. You're here to steal secrets!" Adam Demetrius ran down the corridor toward the elevator. "Well, I'll fix that," he said, pressing the alarm button.

"C'mon," Barney shouted, "we'd better make a run for it!"

Chapter Twelve

BARNEY PEEKED FROM BEHIND THE STAIRWAY AS THE guard walked away from the entrance. "Now's our chance, let's make a move."

He and Cassie hurried toward the exit then dashed out the door. They began running across the back lot then gradually slowed their pace, not wanting to look suspicious.

"Do you think Mr. Demetrius put out an alarm for us?" he asked. "That guy must be crazy to think we'd steal his stuff."

"He's insane," Cassie agreed. "Why would I want to steal his awful bloody eyeballs!"

Barney turned and noticed Mr. Demetrius running after them. "He's still on our trail."

"Thank goodness he's out of shape," said Cassie.

As Adam Demetrius puffed along, Cassie and Barney ducked behind a building. From there, they cut around the soundstage and doubled back. Cassie peeked around the corner, certain they'd finally lost him. Relieved, they ran toward the entrance of soundstage 26. They flashed their VIP badges and the guard allowed them inside.

The crew was finishing up work for the day. Several grips were removing the dolly tracks, flats, and screens. Electricians were repositioning some floodlights and packing up the junction boxes.

"Hey, you sparks," Harvey Winston shouted. "Come here and move this arc light."

A secretary handed out call sheets for the next morning's shooting. The animal trainer was slipping his rats into their cages. "I hope they work tomorrow," he grumbled. "Rats get cranky when they're kept waiting."

"So do I!" Harvey Winston muttered. Exhausted, he threw himself into his chair. "What a rotten day. Two key lights exploded and yesterday's rushes were garbage. Would you believe it! There's a giant *blob* in the background of every shot."

"It's not a blob," said Barney.

"It's The Clump," said Cassie. "It's alive and trying to sabotage this movie."

"That's right," said Barney. "See, Mr. Demetrius accidentally brought the clay creature to life. He was wrong when he thought he'd dumped The Clump."

Wearily, Harvey Winston glanced up. "Are you two back? Haven't I suffered enough?"

"Please listen," said Cassie. "Clump One is hiding out somewhere. Not the big machine, not the actor, the big *clay* clump."

"Hey, you suppose Clump One is jealous of the machine and the actor?" asked Barney. "You think that's why it tried to hurt Fred Fisher? Yeah, maybe that's why it's running around messing up things. It wants to be a movie star, too!"

"Whatever the reason, we've got to stop it," said Cassie. "Professor Ratoff warned us that The Clump is very powerful."

Harvey Winston suddenly seemed interested. "No kidding, tell me more." He listened intently as Cassie and Barney explained the entire situation. "If what you say is true, I think we should close off this set."

"You really *believe* us?" asked Cassie.

"Maybe I do. It's the only sensible explanation for all the crazy things that've been happening. After all, Professor Ratoff is brilliant, so he must know, right?" Harvey Winston placed his arms around the children. "Have you kids told anyone else about this?"

"No one believed us," said Cassie. "Everyone

thinks the accidents are sabotage but we know better."

Winston nodded. "Then this is our secret, right? Don't worry, I'll take care of everything."

"What will you do?" Barney asked.

"First I'll make sure everyone leaves the sound-stage. Then I'll come back and help you trap this creature. You kids sit tight and wait for me, okay?" Harvey Winston patted them both on the back, then hurried away.

Barney felt relieved. "Mr. Winston isn't such a bad guy after all. At last we've got some help."

Gradually, the crew began to leave the soundstage. Two electricians were making a final check on the hydraulic systems of the crane and crab dolly. The photoflood and klieg lights were switched off. Suddenly, the soundstage grew much darker—and strangely silent. All the noise, crowds, and activity of the day were ending.

"This place empties out real fast," Cassie observed uneasily. Within minutes everyone was gone. In the semidarkness the soundstage seemed even larger and more threatening. "Where'd Mr. Winston go?" she wondered.

Once the atmosphere had changed, Barney also felt uneasy. Now everything seemed scary. "He'd better hurry back; I don't like being here alone."

As they waited, Cassie and Barney gradually

realized they *weren't* alone! Someone had sneaked up behind them. A hand reached out of the darkness, quickly grabbing Cassie's arm. She screamed. Barney rushed toward her and bumped into Professor Ratoff. The old man loosened his grip, then spilled a stack of notepapers onto the ground.

Cassie gasped. "Professor? You scared me to death. What're you doing here, how'd you get in?"

"Through the passageway," he explained. "Goodness be thanked I have found you." He stared down at the scattered papers. "Again I have made such a muchly mess," he observed helplessly. "Always my work is in confusion. Could it be part of this wretched curse?"

Barney helped him pick up the papers. "Don't worry, we've found someone who'll help us get rid of the Clump curse."

The professor looked concerned. "Take care, the golem must never know you plan to destroy it. Time has made it cunning. Always it will protect itself. In order to preserve itself it will take orders from anyone, no matter how evil. To destroy it, secret words must be used."

"*What* secret words?" Barney asked.

"Words brought the creature to life and only words can destroy it."

"*Which* words?" asked Cassie.

Professor Ratoff rummaged through his papers, then dropped them again. He knelt down, shuffled them around, and read each one. "You mustn't confront the creature alone. You must have the secret words. I will stay here with you until we find them."

Cassie knew the professor would be more hindrance than help. "Give *us* the words," she suggested. "Where are they written?"

Professor Ratoff glanced over his notes, then pulled his hair in frustration. "On one of these papers—here—or there—or over there perhaps. So many languages, so many incantations, one must surely work."

"Don't you know *which* words to use?" Barney asked.

"I'm not certain," he admitted. "We must have time to experiment." He picked up the papers and shoved them into Barney's hands. "Take them all, but take care," he cautioned. "The creature is devilishly clever."

"Do we say *all* these words?" Barney asked.

"No, you must *write* the words across the creature's forehead. This is the only way to destroy it—the only way."

Barney glanced at the scrawls. "This stuff looks like chicken scratches."

"What foreign language is this?" Cassie asked. She looked up, but the professor had disappeared.

Barney shrugged and shoved the notes in his pocket. "The professor has some nutty ideas. We don't need words, we need action. When Harvey Winston gets back, we can—"

An unexpected thundering noise came echoing through the soundstage. It was a thumping, bumping sound that rattled the ceiling and shook the walls.

It was the sound of giant footsteps approaching.

Cassie and Barney grabbed at each other, afraid to speak.

They knew The Clump must be coming!

Cassie word she saw the huge, but

 Chapter Thirteen

"I TOLD YOU IT WAS REAL!" CASSIE SHOUTED.

Through the dim light, The Clump's huge body cast a shadow across the soundstage wall. It looked hideous! It was ten feet tall and four feet wide: a reddish-brownish lumpy bumpy mess of a thing made from molded clay blobs. Its small mechanical eyes stared blankly. Its mouth was a cavernous, expressionless hole, and when the creature opened it, a terrible noise spilled forth. *Gggrrraaa-rrrggghhh!* It was a thundering, horrifying sound that shook the walls.

Cringing, Barney ran behind a camera. "Help, it's coming, let's get out of here!"

Cassie ran toward the exit. She panicked when she saw the huge metal doors had been locked from the outside. "We're trapped in here, what'll we do?"

"*Gggrrraaarrrggghhh!*" gurgled The Clump, coming closer.

As the creature approached, Barney stared at it. For a moment, he found something comical in the huge clay hulk and felt they might be mistaken about its evil intentions.

"*Gggrrraaarrrggghhh!*" growled The Clump again. It picked up a camera and threw it into the air as if it were a pillow. Barney quickly changed his mind and realized The Clump was out to get them!

Cassie glanced around helplessly, listening to the slow, plodding footsteps move closer. "What happened to Mr. Winston? Do you think The Clump destroyed him? Do you think it knows we're out to get it? The professor warned us about that, remember." She suddenly felt faint. "I think I'm sick."

"Don't pass out or you'll get crunched without a fight," Barney shouted.

Hurrying toward the other end of the soundstage, they hid behind the outdoor set. From there they could watch The Clump approaching.

The creature bumbled along, turning from side to side as if searching for something. Was it looking for *them*? The Clump bumped into lights and cameras, pushing aside everything in its path.

Slowly, it approached the scattered parts of the mechanical Clump machine that lay across the floor. The hulking creature stared at the device with great curiosity. Then, suddenly, The Clump grew furious. It screamed out a great *gggrrraaaggghhh* sound then crunched the machine underfoot. Within moments nothing was left of it but rubble.

"I *told* you it was jealous of that machine," Barney whispered. "I'll bet The Clump wants to be the star of the movie."

The Clump seemed satisfied. But soon it began moving closer to the children's hiding place.

"Look what small eyes the thing has," said Barney. "I'll bet it's almost blind."

"You're right," Cassie agreed. "Maybe it can't *see* us here."

"Then maybe we can *trap* it," Barney suggested, beginning to crawl toward the junction box. "Follow me, okay?"

Only sheer desperation could make Cassie crawl on her stomach, and she was desperate. She bellied her way across the soundstage, maneuvering over yards of cable wires.

Barney was already beside the wall inserting plugs into the junction box. "I watched the electrician do this yesterday. I can handle the equipment."

"What equipment?"

"These are the power lines for the fog, wind,

and rain machines," he explained. "Let's set them off and zap the creature. Since The Clump is made of clay maybe we can turn him into mush."

"Let me help," said Cassie.

Barney passed her a hand-held fog machine. "When The Clump gets closer zap it with this." Then he climbed the ladder toward the rain machine equipment.

The Clump was approaching. Its plodding footsteps shook the soundstage as it moved closer.

"Quick, switch on those machines," Barney shouted from up above.

The Clump heard their voices. It moved faster. It had discovered their hiding place! *"Gggrrraaarrr-ggghhh!"* it shouted, and reached out its lumpy arms.

Cassie switched on the wind machines and turned them toward The Clump. Suddenly, gusty gales of wind began to blow through the fan generators. Their force was so powerful, Cassie leaned against the wall to keep from being swept away.

The Clump drew nearer.

Barney switched on the rain machine pumps. Gallons of water began pouring through the holes in the overhead pipes.

The Clump kept coming closer.

Cassie aimed the hand-held fog machine, pointing the nozzle. The distilled petroleum inside produced a dense smoke that quickly filled the air.

The Clump suddenly stopped in its tracks. It appeared to be weakening.

"We've got it on the run!" Barney shouted triumphantly as he hurried down the ladder. "Now for one final assault." Barney grabbed two respirator masks from a storage bin and threw one toward Cassie. "Here, put this on," he ordered. Then he ran around switching on all the stationary fog machines. Within moments, chunks of dry ice began to make gallons of dense white gaseous vapor, which enveloped the soundstage.

The Clump didn't move.

"We did it!" Barney shouted. "We zapped it!"

But then The Clump began to sway from side to side. Its massive clay body began to pulsate in and out as it breathed the gases. As the water continued to drip down its body, it started to *expand*.

"The water made it grow *bigger*!" Barney gasped.

"And the gas made it *stronger*," said Cassie. "It's *indestructible*."

"*Gggrrraaarrrggghhh!*" The Clump gurgled. It sounded louder and more powerful than ever. With added speed, it lunged toward them.

"We'll never escape now," Cassie moaned, "because it knows we tried to *kill* it."

The Clump was so close, Cassie could *smell* it. It stank of wet, moldy mildewed basements. It dripped red globs of clay over its bumpy warty eyes. It made sloshy thumping noises as it drew closer. It shouted loud angry gurgles and spewed out gaseous fog from its cavernous mouth.

Cassie and Barney were trapped. They cringed in the corner beside a row of klieg lights awaiting their fate.

"I've got one trick left," Barney whispered. He quickly switched on all the kliegs and bathed the soundstage in blinding light.

The Clump stumbled. It covered its eyes. It was stunned.

From behind them Cassie and Barney heard a voice shout out *"Stop!"*

The Clump stopped. *"Gggrrraaarrrggghhh,"* it grumbled one last time, like a record winding down. Then it stood motionless, stiff as a board.

Cassie and Barney turned to see who had ordered The Clump to halt.

It was Harvey Winston, standing at the other end of the soundstage.

"What luck," said Cassie. "Mr. Winston made the creature stop."

They ran toward the director. "We're glad the monster didn't hurt you," said Barney. "We couldn't control it, no matter how we tried."

"It wanted to *kill* us," Cassie shouted.

Harvey Winston remained silent.

"Did you hear us?" asked Barney. "The Clump tried to kill us."

Then Harvey Winston grinned. "I know that," he said.

"You do?" asked Barney.

"Oh, yes. *I* gave The Clump the order to kill you. You see, the creature is in my power now. I am its new *master*!"

Chapter Fourteen

CASSIE AND BARNEY STARED AT THE CLUMP AS IT stood motionless. It looked as if it had turned to stone.

A wildly crazed look came over Harvey Winston. "Unbelievable, isn't it? This monster obeys all my orders. When I tell it to stop, it becomes a statue. It's a director's dream." He approached the creature, stroking its back. "This poor hulk has been hiding so long, it had to tippy-toe around so no one would discover it. But *I* gave it the chance to break free!"

"What's gone wrong with Mr. Winston?" Barney whispered.

"I guess it's like the professor told us," Cassie said. "That creature will take orders from *anyone* in order to preserve itself."

"I should thank you kids for introducing us," raved Harvey Winston. "Naturally I'd heard the rumors about this creature existing, but I never believed them—not until today. When I heard your story I went searching for the monster and found it. Lucky for me, The Clump knew you two were trying to destroy it. That's why it allowed me to become its master. So you see, now *I* am the monster master. Ironic, isn't it?"

"But why did you order the creature to kill us?" asked Cassie.

"Simple," he answered angrily. "Your aunt is connected with Clarion Pictures and I want to destroy Clarion Pictures."

"I knew this was sabotage all along," said Barney, "but why do you want to destroy this studio?"

"Years ago, Gordon Douglas destroyed my father's career. My dad was a stuntman until he got injured on one of G.D.'s movies. He never worked again and Clarion Pictures never paid his medical bills. That's why I didn't care when accidents began happening on this set. Sure, I pretended to be upset, but secretly I hoped it'd push the company toward financial ruin."

"But we're not to blame for that stuff," Barney protested.

"*Everyone* involved with Clarion Pictures is to blame!" Harvey Winston approached The Clump

100

and started to tease it. "Simon says lift up your hands." The giant lump raised its clunky clay arms into the air and held them there. Harvey Winston laughed insanely. "Isn't that a riot? In years of directing, I never had an actor take orders so well. Imagine, I wasted my time working with no-talents when this specimen was available!"

"What are you going to do with it?" asked Cassie nervously.

"Order it to *kill* you both," he replied. "When the crew returns in the morning, they'll find your crushed bodies on this soundstage. It'll be another tragic accident. But Clarion Pictures won't be able to hush up this one like all the others. They'll have to close down the studio forever. David Douglas will go bankrupt, and I'll finally have my revenge!"

"Quit kidding. You wouldn't order that creature to kill us, would you?" asked Barney.

"You couldn't do a thing like that, could you?" asked Cassie.

"Sure I could. It's a foolproof plan. No one else knows the monster exists. Everyone will blame David Douglas for not taking proper safety measures."

"Professor Ratoff knows all about the monster," Cassie reminded him.

"But everyone thinks he's crazy. No one believes a crazy person!" Harvey Winston began to laugh hysterically.

Barney glanced at The Clump standing motionless as a stone statue. Then he glanced at Harvey Winston still laughing like a nut. He knew it was the perfect time to escape. But where? As his eyes searched around, Barney noticed a glimmer of light from the opposite end of the soundstage—a faint red glow emerging from an opening. Suddenly he remembered the professor had told them he'd come through a passageway. "There must be an exit back there," he whispered.

Harvey Winston kept laughing insanely.

The Clump continued to stand motionless.

"We've become the slaves of a monster and a madman!" Cassie gasped.

"No, we're making a run for it," said Barney, grabbing her arm.

They dashed across the soundstage then hurried toward the glimmer of light in the distance.

"Come back, you can't escape," Harvey Winston shouted. "The creature will catch you!"

"Don't turn around," said Barney, racing ahead.

As he'd supposed, there was an exit at the other end of the soundstage and the door led into a huge dark passageway.

"Where does this lead?" asked Cassie.

"Who cares? It's our only escape."

As they hurried down the long passage, they could hear The Clump following behind them.

The underpass was a long, snaky tunnel that led back into the special effects laboratory.

"This place must go around in circles," said Cassie.

"I guess this tunnel is used to move the special effects onto the soundstage," said Barney. "Mr. Demetrius likes to keep his projects secret."

"And I'll bet this is where The Clump has been hiding," said Cassie. "No wonder nobody discovered it."

Barney paused before entering the corridor leading to the labs. He could hear The Clump's slow, plodding footsteps moving through the tunnel. *"Gggrrraaarrrggghhh!"* its voice echoed, bouncing off the walls.

"Let's hurry," said Cassie, "it'll be here soon with orders to kill us."

Barney opened the door and ran down the hall. "Maybe we could try to blow it up," he suggested. "Mr. Demetrius keeps explosives in the lab. Should we ask him to help us?" All the doors were locked. In desperation, they ran toward the foam lab. "I forgot everyone's gone home already," said Barney, "but maybe there's something in here we could zap the creature with."

The Clump had already caught up with them. It came bursting into the foam lab, crunching the door underfoot.

Barney refused to surrender. As the monster approached, he lured it into the huge walk-in oven that was used for curing rubber. "Slam that door, Cassie," he shouted, then he switched on the heat. He turned the dials as far as they would go, up to one thousand degrees. "If we can't blow it up, maybe we can cook it."

Heat waves quickly began rising inside the giant oven. The Clump started banging against the heavily insulated walls.

"Do you think it's melting?" asked Cassie.

"Sure, nothing could survive such heat."

But suddenly the huge oven door came smashing open and The Clump emerged, angrier than ever. Its clay body was burning hot and smoke was pouring from its mouth.

"Now it's madder than ever," said Cassie. "You shouldn't have baked it."

"I guess *nothing* can stop it," said Barney.

"Wait," shouted Cassie, "we forgot the *secret words*." She pulled the papers from Barney's pocket. "Professor Ratoff said one of these incantations would destroy the creature."

"But which one? There are dozens of them. Besides, that monster won't let us write on its forehead; it's hopeless!"

104

As The Clump came toward them, Cassie noticed the intense heat had melted big globs of clay over its beady eyes. "Look, it's blinder than ever. You think you can lure it into that spray-paint booth?"

"I'll try," said Barney.

The spray-paint booth was enclosed by glass on three sides with a center opening. It was used to paint the mannequins and dummies used in special effects shots, so it was very large. Luckily, it was large enough for The Clump to enter.

Barney banged against the glass walls to attract the monster's attention. He lured it closer. As The Clump lunged forward to catch Barney, it stumbled into the booth instead.

"Think fast, Cassie, it won't stay in there for long."

"Get to the paint guns," she shouted, throwing half the notes to Barney.

Outside the spray-paint booth, dozens of aerosol paint guns were lined in rows. Cassie and Barney began pressing them all. Giant squirts of paint shot out toward the booth. They sprayed out all the words until The Clump's huge body was covered in letters.

The Clump looked dazed. It growled, grunted, gasped, and groaned. Then it flailed its arms against the sides of the spray booth, shattering the glass.

Now The Clump was loose and lunging forward.

Cassie and Barney held their ground. They knew the spray guns were the only weapon they had left, so they kept spraying out every word written on the papers.

Within minutes, The Clump looked like walking graffiti. Words were sprayed across its back and front. Words covered its entire blobby face. Every time it growled its *gggrrraaarrrggghhh*, more words got sprayed inside its mouth. Red, yellow, green, orange, blue, black—every color word, every language, every incantation.

But The Clump was still alive!

"We'd better make a run for it," said Barney. "This isn't working."

Cassie refused to abandon the spray guns. "No, keep trying," she insisted. She gave the creature one final blast and sprayed the last words written on the crumpled paper.

At last the creature seemed to weaken.

The Clump stumbled. It swayed back and forth, heaving its giant moldy mass of clay flesh.

The Clump's tiny beady eyes receded even farther into its blobby face. The ground shook as its massive legs began to wobble. Then suddenly its clay arms began to crack. It turned a dark reddish brown as if it were drying up. Then its arms began to crumble into pieces.

"It's beginning to fall apart!" Barney shouted. "The secret words worked. We're safe."

"We're not safe yet," Cassie warned him, "watch out!"

The clay creature opened its mouth. It gurgled out one final raspy *gggrrraaarrrrggghhhhhhhhhhh-hhhhhhh*—then its head fell over to one side. Suddenly, it began to separate from the body. The head crashed to the ground, toppling everything in its path.

Cassie and Barney quickly moved away as the creature's broken body parts started hurtling toward them. They hurried down the corridor, afraid to look back. When they'd reached the exit door, they reentered the passageway.

It was dark and deadly silent inside the passage.

"Do you think The Clump is really dead?" asked Cassie nervously.

"Sure, we watched it fall apart."

Despite what they'd seen, Cassie feared the creature might still be indestructible. "Let's hide in here for a while just in case."

As Cassie leaned against the wall, a hand emerged from the darkness. She screamed as the hand grabbed at Barney's throat.

It was Harvey Winston, and he looked crazier than ever.

"Where's The Clump?" he shouted. "It should've

destroyed you two by now. *I'm* its master and I ordered it to destroy you both."

Choking for breath, Barney pushed him aside. "Leave us alone," he pleaded.

Together, he and Cassie raced through the underpass.

Harvey Winston raced after them. "Stop, you must take my *direction!*" he shouted wildly.

At the other end of the underpass, Barney locked and bolted the door behind them. "Winston can't grab us now."

Cassie glanced around uneasily. "Maybe not, but we've cut ourselves off from the only other exit. The soundstage entrance is locked, so how will we get out of here?"

Cassie and Barney shuddered. They heard *noises.*

Someone was moving across the darkened soundstage.

Someone was clattering and banging things.

Someone was coming closer!

"Oh, no!" Cassie gasped. "The Clump must be back. Now we're really trapped!"

Chapter Fifteen

"IT'S NOT POSSIBLE," SAID BARNEY. "THE CLUMP couldn't put itself back together again."

"It *did*," Cassie argued. "What'll we do now? Crazy Mr. Winston is waiting for us down there and The Clump is waiting for us up here."

"We'll hide," said Barney, slowly creeping across the soundstage toward the living room set. There, he and Cassie crawled under a tapestry thrown over an oak table.

They sat, barely breathing, as the footsteps approached.

Cassie closed her eyes. She didn't want to watch herself be crushed by The Clump's huge blobby feet. "It wants revenge," she whispered. "You shouldn't have cooked it. It came back to life because you *baked* it."

"It came back because you *sprayed* it," Barney argued. He peeked out from underneath the tapestry but he didn't see the creature.

Someone was coming closer but it wasn't The Clump.

Cassie looked, too. "I see two feet out there but they're not huge blobby ones."

"It's a *woman*," Barney whispered. "Who is she? How'd she get in here?"

As the figure drew nearer, Cassie noticed something familiar. "Aunt Alex has those same shoes."

"Those same feet, too," Barney added, sneaking a bigger peek. "It *is* Aunt Alex. What's *she* doing here?"

Barney began to crawl free.

But then Aunt Alex spoke.

"Basil," she called out, "are you here? I'm waiting for you."

Cassie pulled Barney back. "How embarrassing. We can't let Aunt Alex know we're here. I think we've stumbled into her rendezvous."

"Her what?"

"Her romantic meeting, stupid. Aunt Alex must've arranged a tryst with Basil Trelawny. I guess that means she's more than just his old fan, she must be his *old flame*."

110

"What bunk, I'm going out there." As Barney began to crawl from under the table, he noticed Basil Trelawny approaching.

One solitary klieg light silhouetted the two figures against the wall. Basil kissed Aunt Alex on the cheek.

"See, I told you," said Cassie, pulling Barney back.

Barney sat sulking. "No, she can't love that old guy. Aunt Al is always telling us how much she loved *Hugo.*" Barney felt strangely betrayed. He didn't want to see Aunt Alex now—it was far too embarrassing.

Cassie clung to every word they said, absolutely fascinated.

"Dear Alexandra, I'm so glad you could come," said Basil Trelawny. "This place has such memories for us both, doesn't it?"

"Yes," Aunt Alex agreed. "This soundstage is where you made your movie debut."

"And where I lost my one and only love," Basil added. "If I hadn't been so involved in my career, I would've proposed to you all those years ago. Losing you was the biggest mistake of my life. I'll never forgive myself. Have you forgiven me? Have you had a happy life?"

"A very happy life," said Aunt Alex. "My late husband, Hugo, was a wonderful man. So don't live in the past, Basil. What happened between us was more than forty years ago. We've both changed a lot since then."

"No, your face is etched on my heart. It will *never* change."

"But I've grown so old."

"Only more lovely," Basil insisted. He stared into Aunt Alex's eyes. "Yes, this is the real you I've imagined so often, only you're more beautiful than ever."

Barney couldn't take much more. "This conversation is *putrid*."

Cassie stifled a sob. "It's the best *affaire d'amour* I've ever heard. Isn't it ironic? Aunt Alex kept trying to change herself but Basil loves her just the way she is." Cassie blew her nose.

It was a very loud blow and Aunt Alex heard it! She pushed away the tapestry and peered underneath the table. "Who on earth is under there?" she asked.

Before Cassie or Barney could reply, the huge entrance doors of the soundstage swung open. Suddenly, all the kliegs and photofloods were switched on. Then a voice called out, "Who's in here? Speak up!"

Crenshaw came rushing through the door. He was followed by the chauffeur who was followed by Adam Demetrius who was followed by David Douglas.

"*I'm* in here," Aunt Alex shouted, "but I don't know who's under *there*. Come out at once."

Cassie and Barney crawled out from underneath the table.

Aunt Alex was very surprised. "What are you two doing here?" She stared at Crenshaw. "Did you send the children out spying again? Honestly, Ollie, I can't understand your behavior. Ever since we arrived in Hollywood, you've been acting strangely."

"*Me? You're* the one," Crenshaw protested. "*I* didn't know the children were in here."

"Sorry, I had to tell Mr. Crenshaw where I took you kids," the chauffeur explained. "I didn't mean to get you into trouble."

"I'll bet the children have gotten themselves into trouble," said Aunt Alex.

"Right, those kids are spies," Adam Demetrius argued. "They admitted it. They're responsible for ruining my lab. The foam room is a wreck—paint sprayed all over the place."

David Douglas glanced around the soundstage. "Everything in here is wrecked, too. You're right, we've been sabotaged." He stared at Cassie and Barney. "You two are responsible for all this vandalism."

"No, The Clump did it," Barney argued.

"The what?"

"The Clump," said Cassie. "The Clump wrecked everything. But don't worry, we killed it."

"You what?"

"We killed it," said Barney. "First we blew it, then we drowned it, then we gassed it, then we smoked it."

"But it wouldn't die," Cassie continued, "so we blinded it and then we baked it."

"But it still wouldn't die," said Barney, "not until Cassie sprayed it."

Aunt Alex leaned over to feel their foreheads. "They don't seem ill but they sound delirious."

"No, there was a real monster and we destroyed it," Barney insisted.

Aunt Alex smiled patiently. "What kind of monster was it, dear?"

Basil Trelawny looked confused. "Do these children belong to you, Alexandra?"

"Yes, they're my grandniece and grandnephew and generally, they're quite sensible."

"There *was* a monster," Cassie insisted.

David Douglas hurried around the soundstage taking inventory of the damages. "The lights, camera, sets, most everything is smashed. And there's water damage, too. Who turned on that rain machine?"

"I did," Barney admitted.

"My lab looks the same way," said Adam Demetrius. "Like a bulldozer went through it."

David Douglas leaned against an overturned camera. "I need my stomach pills," he moaned.

In the midst of the chaos, Professor Ratoff arrived. Ignoring the destruction, he hurried to Cassie and Barney. "Are you both all right? Some terrible feeling I had; yes, I feared for you both. You must not try to defeat the golem alone. Promise me you will forget such a wild plan."

"We did defeat it," said Barney proudly. "It's dead. We killed it with your secret words."

"Trouble is, no one will believe us," Cassie said. "They think *we* caused this giant mess."

"Mr. Demetrius thinks we're vandals," Barney added.

From the other end of the soundstage, David Douglas began shouting. "Oh, no, this is dreadful! This is terrible! This is *hopeless!*"

Everyone ran to see what was wrong. There, they discovered David Douglas standing over the broken parts of the ruined Clump machine. The mechanical monster was totally demolished.

"My million-dollar investment is destroyed," he moaned. "I can't afford to rebuild the Clump machine. We have no movie without a Clump! No

115

movie, no revenues. No revenues, no studio. I'm *ruined*, down the tubes!"

"The Clump killed that machine," Barney explained.

"I think it was jealous," Cassie added. "It wanted to be the star of the movie itself."

"No, you kids are to blame for everything," said Adam Demetrius.

"That's right," David Douglas agreed, "you kids admitted killing The Clump."

"We didn't mean *that* Clump," said Barney. "We told you, the monster killed that Clump."

"And we killed the monster," Cassie added.

David Douglas started pulling his hair. "Stop talking crazy, there is no monster."

"Not anymore," said Barney, "but there was. Mr. Demetrius made it."

"Yes, you're always talking about making your fancy machines more powerful," said David Douglas. "Are you responsible for all this, Demetrius? Did a machine run amok?"

"Don't blame me for this," said Mr. Demetrius. "I told you it was all *their* fault."

"You're right," David Douglas agreed. "I want you brats off my property immediately."

"How dare you," said Aunt Alex. "No one speaks to these children like that, *no one*. I've no idea who caused this vandalism, but Cassie and

Barney would never be so destructive. It must be some horrible mistake." She glanced at them both. "It's time you told us exactly what happened here—the entire truth."

Professor Ratoff drew Cassie and Barney aside. "You must never reveal the whole truth," he whispered. "None must know the golem was brought to life. None must learn the secret words. In the wrong hands, such knowledge would bring much destruction. More golems would be built. More greedy people would become their masters. So you must never tell. This must be our secret, forever and always."

"Forever?" asked Cassie.

"And *always*," he said solemnly.

Aunt Alex approached the children. "What have you to say for yourselves?"

Cassie and Barney looked at all the faces staring at them, all waiting for a sensible explanation.

"Tell us everything that happened here," said Crenshaw.

What *had* happened? Cassie wondered. Now that it was over, she wasn't sure. Had The Clump been a mechanical creation that had worn down? Or had it been a monster destroyed by the professor's secret words?

Cassie didn't know. "Perhaps there was an earthquake," she suggested.

117

Across the soundstage, a loud banging came from the exit door leading to the underpass. "Let me out of here!" a voice demanded.

"Someone must be trapped in the passageway," said Adam Demetrius. He ran to the door and unlocked it.

Harvey Winston emerged. He looked wild-eyed and half crazed. He pushed everyone aside then started screaming, "I am the monster master! Make way for the monster master!"

"What happened to *him*?" asked Crenshaw.

David Douglas frantically pulled at his hair. "It's the movie business," he shouted. "Sooner or later it makes everyone go crazy!"

Chapter Sixteen

"WELL, ARE YOU OR NOT?" ASKED BARNEY. "CASSIE says you are but I say you're not, so who's right?"

Crenshaw didn't answer. He was stretched out on a lounge chair beside the hotel pool sunning himself.

Cassie glanced at Crenshaw's wildly patterned swim trunks. She looked at his sunglasses and large straw hat, deciding he looked just like a movie mogul. "One of us has to be right, so which is it?"

"Tell us," Barney insisted. "Are you in love with Aunt Alex or not?"

"I've worked for your great-aunt for thirty years," he replied, "and I've come to respect and admire her greatly."

"That's no answer," said Cassie.

"It's the only one you'll get, young lady. My personal feelings aren't your affair. Haven't you both snooped enough?"

"I liked being a spy," said Barney, "except for the scary parts. Only I'm not sure what we learned."

"We learned you were all wrong about Angela Marley," Cassie reminded him. "I told you she was innocent." Cassie applied some suntan lotion, then lay on her lounge. It gave her great satisfaction to know she'd been Angela's defender.

"And you were wrong about Basil Trelawny," said Barney. Then he watched Aunt Alex emerge from the pool. "You aren't in love with that old guy, are you, Aunt Al?"

"Watch who you call old," she said, then wrapped herself up in a towel and sat down.

"Well, you aren't in love with him, are you?"

Aunt Alex smiled. "As *my* aunt always told me, it's none of your beeswax." She stretched out on her lounge. "I hope poor Mr. Winston recovers quickly. Maybe you children should send him a get-well card."

"No, thanks," said Cassie, "not after he tried to kill us."

"Winston will be all right," said Crenshaw reassuringly. "A few months of therapy and he'll be back to normal. If there's one thing Hollywood has lots of, it's psychiatrists." He felt his nose begin to peel so he pushed his straw hat over it. "Wasn't that a wild story Winston told? Naturally, he was trying to cover up for sabotaging the set, but imagine telling everyone there was a real monster loose on the soundstage."

"Yeah, imagine," said Barney. He was determined to keep his promise to Professor Ratoff.

"No wonder David Douglas tried to hush things up," said Crenshaw. "But the news is out now. All the papers have the story about the jinxed set at Clarion Pictures."

Barney nudged Cassie. "You promised the professor you wouldn't tell," he whispered.

"I didn't tell anything," Cassie protested.

"Then who did?" asked Barney.

"Harvey Winston blabbed everything," Crenshaw explained. "Naturally, no one believed his crazy story. But I called in all the reporters anyway."

"*You* did?" asked Cassie. "Why?"

Aunt Alex flipped up her sunglasses. "Because Ollie is a shrewd businessman," she explained. "And because now that I'm the new owner of Clarion Pictures, he wants the studio to make tons of money."

"When did *you* buy Clarion Pictures?" Barney asked.

"This morning," Aunt Alex said. "David Douglas was anxious to sell, so I got a good price."

"A *very* good price," said Crenshaw proudly. "I handled the deal personally."

"That's a lousy business deal," said Barney. "The soundstage is ruined and the mechanical monster is a wreck. You'll spend a fortune for repairs."

Crenshaw laughed. "David Douglas thought that, too, but that's because he has no business sense. Know what you need in business, young man? Courage and imagination."

"And you have *both*," said Aunt Alex admiringly. "Ollie, tell the children your secret formula for success."

"*Advertise*," said Crenshaw. "You see, all these months David Douglas hushed up the problems on the set. Not me! I *advertised* them. All the papers will carry the story and Clarion Pictures will get a fortune's worth of free publicity."

"But no one believed Harvey Winston's story," said Barney.

"It doesn't matter," said Crenshaw. "When the movie comes out, everyone will want to see it anyway. They'll be curious, so we're guaranteed to make a fortune. Yessir, this time next year Alex will be swimming in film profits."

"But Aunt Alex doesn't approve of horror movies," Cassie argued.

"You're absolutely right," she agreed, "so we're returning to Professor Ratoff's original script. We'll make a quality movie with a quality actor. It will introduce a whole new generation to the marvelous talents of Basil Trelawny."

Crenshaw agreed. "Yessir, it will make him a star all over again. This time next year everyone will know the name of Basil Trelawny."

"And he'll have *you* to thank," said Aunt Alex. She leaned over and kissed Crenshaw on the cheek. "What would I do without you?"

"I don't know, I'm sure," he answered, blushing.

"But what about Angela Marley?" asked Cassie with concern. "Does the original script have a part in it for her, too?"

"Certainly," said Crenshaw. "It's a much bigger, juicier part. Miss Marley was so pleased with the script change, she invited us all over to her trailer for lunch this afternoon."

Cassie was thrilled. She, too, felt like kissing Crenshaw—but she quickly stifled the impulse.

"I don't get it," said Barney. "If everything was such a big mess, how could it all work out so great?"

Aunt Alex smiled. "Maybe it's because we're in

Hollywood. They say everything out here is an *illusion*."

Not everything, Cassie thought. Her meeting with Angela Marley would be *real*. She'd get Angela's autograph and take pictures with her, too. When Cassie returned to boarding school, she'd have real memories to bring along. Real memories that would, hopefully, last a lifetime.

Barney wasn't sure what to think. Had The Clump been an evil monster or a mechanical creation? If it was a monster, did it destroy the machine out of jealousy? And who was secretly in love with whom? Did it matter?

"I guess you're right," he agreed. "Nothing is real out here in Hollywood."

"Except the sunshine," said Aunt Alex.

"And the movie stars," said Cassie.

"And the movie profits," Crenshaw added.

"And room service," said Barney. Then he relaxed on his lounge and closed his eyes.